A Christmas Beginning

A Christmas Beginning

A Novel

Anne Perry

OUACHITA TECHNICAL COLLEGE

BALLANTINE BOOKS · NEW YORK

Copyright © 2007 by Anne Perry

Published in the United States by Ballantine Books, an imprint of The Random House Publishing Group, a division of Random House, Inc., New York.

BALLANTINE and colophon are registered trademarks of Random House, Inc.

Library of Congress Cataloging-in-Publication Data

Perry, Anne.
A Christmas beginning : a novel / Anne Perry.
p. cm.
ISBN-13: 978-0-345-48582-3 (acid-free paper)
ISBN-10: 0-345-48582-3 (acid-free paper)
1. Murder—Fiction. 2. Anglesey (Wales)—Fiction. 3. Aristocracy (Social class)—Fiction. 4. Great Britain—History—Victoria, 1837–1901—Fiction. 5. Christmas stories. I. Title.

PR6066.E693C465 2007
823'.914—dc22
2007026444

Printed in the United States of America

Map © Mapping Specialists, Ltd., Madison, WI, U.S.A.

www.ballantinebooks.com

2 4 6 8 9 7 5 3 1

First Edition

Text design by Julie Schroeder

To all those who
dream impossible dreams

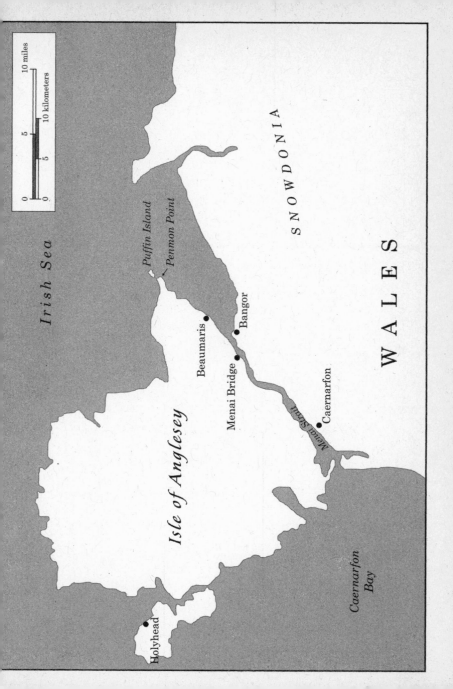

A Christmas Beginning

*S*O THIS WAS THE ISLE OF ANGLESEY. RUNCORN stood on the rugged headland and stared across the narrow water of the Menai Strait towards the mountains of Snowdonia and mainland Wales, and he wondered why on earth he had chosen to come here, alone in December. The air was hard, ice-edged, and laden with the salt of the sea. Runcorn was a Londoner, used to the rattle of hansom cabs on the cobbles, the gas lamps gleaming in the afternoon dusk. Every day he was surrounded by the sing-song voices of costermongers, the cries of news vendors, drivers of every kind of vehicle—broughams to drays—and the air carried the smell of smoke and manure.

This isolated island must be the loneliest place in Britain, all bare hills and hard, bright water, and silence except for the moan of the wind in the grass. The black skeleton of the Menai Bridge had a certain grace, but it was a cold elegance, not the low, familiar arches across the Thames. The few lights flickering on in the town of Beaumaris behind him indicated nothing like the vast city he was used to, teeming with the passions, the sorrow, and the dreams of millions.

Of course the reason he was here was simple. Runcorn had nowhere else in particular to be for Christmas, no family. He lived alone. He knew many people, but they were colleagues rather than friends. He had earned his promotions until he was now, at fifty, a senior superintendent in the Metropolitan Police, separated by office from those he had once worked beside. But he was not a gentleman, like those of his own rank. He had not the polish, the confidence, the ease of speech and grace of movement that comes with not having to care what people thought of you.

He smiled to himself as the wind stung his face. Monk, his colleague many years ago, one of his few friends, had not been born a gentleman either, but

4

somehow he had always managed to seem like one. That used to hurt, but it did not anymore. He knew that Monk was human too, and vulnerable. He could make mistakes. And perhaps Runcorn himself was wiser.

The last case in which they had worked together had been difficult and in the end ugly. Now Runcorn was tired of the city and he was due several weeks of leave. Why not take it somewhere as different as possible? He would refresh his mind away from the familiar and predictable, take long walks in the open, think deeply for a change.

The sun was sinking in the southwest, shedding brilliant, burning light over the water. The land was dark as the color faded and the headlands jutted purple and black out of the sea. Only the uplands, ribbed pale like crumpled velvet, still caught the last rays of light.

How long was winter twilight here? Would he soon find himself lost, unable to see the way back to his lodgings? It was bitterly cold already. His feet were numb from standing. Turning, he started to walk towards the east and the darkening sky. What was there to think about? He was good at his job, patient, possibly a little pedestrian. He never had flashes of brilliant intuition, but he got where he needed to. He had succeeded far more than any of the other young men who had started when he had. In fact, his own success had surprised him.

But was he happy?

That was a stupid question, as if happiness were something you could own and have for always. He was happy at times, as for example when a case was closed and he knew he had done it well, found a difficult truth and left no doubts to haunt him afterwards, no savage and half-answered questions.

He was happy when he sat down by the fire at the end of a long day, took the weight off his feet, and ate something really good, like a thick-crusted ham-and-egg pie, or hot sausages with mashed potatoes. He liked good music, even classical music sometimes, although he would not admit it, in case people thought he was putting on airs. And he liked dogs. A good dog always made him smile. Was that enough?

He could only just see the road at his feet now. He thought about the huge bridge behind him, spanning the whole surge and power of the sea. What about the man who built that? Had he been happy? He had certainly created something to marvel at, and changed the lives of people far into the future.

Runcorn had untangled a few problems, but had he ever built anything, or did he always use other people's bridges? Where did he go, anyway? No more than home to bed. Tonight it was to be an unfamiliar lodging house. It was comfortable. He would sleep well, he usually did. Certainly it was warm enough, and Mrs. Owen was an agreeable woman, generous in nature.

*T*he next morning was sharp and cold, but a pale sun struggled over the horizon, milky soft through a fine veil of cloud, which Mrs. Owen assured him would burn off soon. The frost was only a dusting of white here and there, enough to make the hollows stand out on the long, uneven lawn stretching down to the big yew tree.

Runcorn ate a hearty breakfast, talked with Mrs.

Owen for a little while because it was only civil to appear interested as she told him about some of the local places and customs. Afterwards he set out to walk again.

This time he headed uphill, climbing steadily until nearly midday when he turned and gazed out at a cloudless sky, and a sea shimmering unbroken into the distance.

He stood there for some time, lost in the enormity of it, then gradually descended. He was on the outskirts of Beaumaris again when he turned a corner in the road and came face-to-face with a tall, slender man of unusual elegance, even in his heavy, winter coat and hat. He was in his mid-thirties, handsome, clean-shaven. They both stopped, staring at each other. The man blinked, uncertain except recognizing Runcorn's face as familiar.

Runcorn knew him instantly, as if it had been only a week ago they had met. But it was longer than that, much longer. It had been a case of suicide suspected to be a murder. John Barclay had lived in a house backing onto the mews where the body had been found. It was not Barclay whom Runcorn remembered; it was his widowed sister, Melisande Ewart. Even standing here in the middle of this bright, windy road, Runcorn could see her face as clearly as if it were she who were here now, not her arrogant, unhelpful brother.

"Excuse me," Barclay said tensely, stepping around Runcorn as if they had been strangers and walking on up the road, lengthening his stride. But Runcorn had seen the recognition in his face, and the distaste.

Was Melisande here too? If she was, he might see her, or at least catch a glimpse. Did she still look the same? Was the curve of her hair as soft? The way she smiled and the sadness in her had continued to haunt him in the year since they'd last met.

It was ridiculous for him to think of her still. If she remembered him at all, it would be as a policeman determined to do his job regardless of fear or favor, but with possibly a modicum of kindness. It was her courage, her defiance of her brother Barclay in identifying the corpse and taking the witness stand, that had closed the case. He had always wondered how much that had cost her afterwards in Barclay's displeasure. There had been nothing he could do to help.

He began walking again, around the bend in the road and past the first house of the village. Was she staying here also? He quickened his step without re-alizing it. The sun was bright, the frost nothing more than sparkling drops in the grass.

How could he find out if she was here, without being overeager? He could hardly ask, as if they were social acquaintances. He was a policeman who had investigated a death. It would be pointless to see her, and much too painful. Chastising himself, he thought what a fool he was to have even thought about it.

He hurried on towards his lodgings, the safety of Mrs. Owen's dining room table and the cheerful con-versation of strangers.

*B*ut Runcorn did not stop thinking of Melisande. The weather grew a little milder, and for the first time it was well above freezing. He saw more than a hundred birds pecking over a field, and a farmer told him they were redwings. There were plenty of yellow gorse in bloom and the occasional cowslip. He walked in the sun and the wind, once or twice in the rain, and over a couple of days learned his way along the shore to east and west of Beaumaris. He found favorite places, hollows out of the wind, orchids that caught his breath with sudden pleasure, intimate rock pools where strange shells and seaweeds could be found.

On Sunday he dressed in the one decent suit he had brought with him and went to the morning service at the church nearest to the place in the road where he had encountered John Barclay. It was a solid stone building with stained-glass windows and a bell that rang out in the gusty air, the rich sound carrying across the town and into the fields beyond.

Runcorn knew why he was here, drawn as if by the pull of a magnet. It had nothing to do with the worship of God, even though he entered through the great, carved wooden doors with head bowed, hat in his hand, and a mixture of reverence and hope that made his heart beat faster.

Inside the old church was a stone floor and a high ceiling crossed with massive, carved hammer beams. The light was hazy and the sound hushed. Colors in the great illuminated windows showed the stations of the cross and what looked like a woman following after the figure of Christ in the street. She knelt to touch his robe, and Runcorn remembered a biblical story about healing. He could not recall the details.

The congregation was already seated as he slipped into a pew along one side. He watched with interest, bowing his head as Barclay passed by him, then lifting it again with a sudden pang of disappointment that Melisande was not with him. But there was no reason for her to be on this wind-scoured island in its barren glory, with its wild coast, its birds, and the roaring sea. What was there for a beautiful woman to do here?

Then another, entirely different woman, perhaps in her mid-twenties, walked past the end of his pew and continued on up the aisle. She moved with a unique grace, almost fluid, as if she were not touching the hard stone of a church floor with her boots, but were barefoot on grass, or the smooth sand of a beach. Her head was high, and when she turned, her pale face was quickened by a secret laughter, as if she understood something no one else did. She was wearing a green so somber it appeared almost black, and her cloud of dark hair escaped the rather rakish hat she seemed to have put on at the last moment, without thought. Her eyes were peat-brown, and wide. Runcorn noticed that, even though she looked at him for only an instant.

She went on up to the very front row, and sat down beside a woman perhaps fifteen years older, who turned to greet her with a quick, warm smile.

Runcorn suddenly noticed the movement of a man a couple of rows in front of him who quickly turned to stare at the younger woman with an intensity unsuitable in church. His features were regular and he had an excellent head of hair, thick with a slightly auburn tone to it. He was almost handsome, but for a tightness about his mouth that gave him a look of meanness. He was perhaps approaching forty.

If the young woman were aware of the man's attention, she showed no sign of it at all; indeed, she seemed indifferent to any of the people around her except the vicar who now appeared. Middle-aged, he had a pale, ascetic face with a high brow and the same peat-dark eyes as the girl in green. Almost immediately the service commenced, with the usual soothing and familiar ritual. The vicar conducted the proceedings somberly and somewhat as if it was a habit he was so accustomed to that it required far less than his full attention. Runcorn began to wonder if there were any way in which he could escape before the sermon without his departure being rudely obvious, and concluded that there was not. Instead, he decided to occupy his thoughts by looking at the people.

The man in front of Runcorn was turning to look at the young woman again. There was too much emotion in his face to believe he was simply admiring her. He had to know her, and there had to have been conflict between them, at least on his part.

What of her? Runcorn could not see her now because she was facing forward, her attention on the vicar as he began his sermon. His subject was obedience, an easy matter for which to find plenty of reference, though not one so simple to give life to or warmth, or to make seem relevant to Christmas, now less than two weeks away. Runcorn wondered why on earth the vicar had chosen it, for it was singularly inappropriate. But then, Runcorn reflected, he did not know the congregation. There could be all kinds of passions running out of control that obedience might hold in check. The vicar might be the good shepherd trying every way he knew to lead wayward sheep to safe pasture.

Barclay was also looking at the young woman in green, and for a moment there was a hunger in his face that was quite unmistakable. Runcorn was almost embarrassed to have seen it. Two men courting the same woman? Well, this must happen in every village in England.

He had not been paying attention to the service. He had no idea what the curate had risen to do, only that his face was in every way different from that of the vicar. Where the older man was studious and disciplined, this man seemed mercurial and full of dreams. Though barely into his twenties, there was a keen intelligence in him. He looked at the girl and smiled, then as if caught in a minor offense, quickly

15

looked away. She turned a little, and Runcorn could see, even in the brief profile of her face, that she was smiling back, not wistfully as a lover, but with life and laughter, as a friend.

Runcorn would never know what tangle of emotions bound those people together. He had come to church because he thought Barclay would be here and, in spite of the absurdity of it, there might be a chance he would see Melisande. He would like to think she was happy, whatever it was that had saddened her in London. The thought of her still facing some sort of darkness was so heavy inside him he felt tight in his chest, as if a physical band prevented him from taking a full breath. Where was she? He could not possibly ask Barclay if she was well. And any answer he gave would be no more than a formality. His ilk did not discuss health or happiness with tradesmen, and he had made it abundantly clear that he regarded Runcorn, and all police, as the refuse collectors of society. He had said as much.

The congregation rose again to sing another hymn. The organist was good and the music pealed out with a powerful, joyous melody. Runcorn enjoyed singing, his voice was rich and he knew how to carry a tune.

It was as he started to sit down again, a moment or two after the people to the left of him, that he saw Melisande. She was nowhere near Barclay, but it was unmistakably her. He could never forget her face, the gentleness in it, the clear eyes, the laughter and the pain so near the surface.

She looked at him now with sudden, wide amazement. She smiled, and then self-consciously turned away.

Runcorn's heart lurched, the room swayed around him, and he sat down in the pew so hard the woman in front turned to glare at him.

Melisande was here! And she remembered him! That smile was far more than just the acknowledgment of a stranger caught staring at her. It was more than civility, it had had warmth. He could feel it burn inside him.

The rest of the service passed by him in a blur of sound, beautiful and meaningless, like the splashes of color the sunlight painted through the windows.

Afterwards he stood in the bright winter stillness

as the congregation came outside again, talking to each other, shaking the vicar by the hand, milling around exchanging gossip and good wishes.

Someone recognized him as a stranger and invited him to be introduced. He moved forward without thought as to what he was going to say, and found himself shaking the hand of the vicar, Reverend Arthur Costain, and offering his name but not his police rank.

"Welcome to Anglesey, Mr. Runcorn," Costain said with a smile. "Are you staying with us over Christmas, or perhaps we may hope you will be with us longer?"

In that instant Runcorn made his decision. Melisande and Barclay already knew his profession, but he would tell no one else. He was not ashamed of it, but knowledge that he was a policeman made many people uncomfortable, and their defense was to avoid him.

"I will stay as long as I can," he replied. "Certainly until the New Year."

Costain seemed pleased. "Excellent. Perhaps you will call at the vicarage some time. My wife and I would be delighted to make your better acquaintance." He indicated the woman beside him, who had turned to welcome the girl in green during the service. Upon closer inspection, she was more interesting than he could have guessed from several rows behind. She was not as beautiful as her younger companion, but there was a strength in her face which was unusual, full of both humor and patience. Runcorn found it instantly pleasing, and accepted the invitation, only then realizing that the vicar, at least, had said it as a matter of form. Runcorn blushed at his own foolishness.

It was Mrs. Costain who rescued him. "Forgive my husband, Mr. Runcorn. He is always hoping for new parishioners. We shall not press you into staying beyond your pleasure, I assure you. Is this your first visit to the island?"

He recognized her kindness with surprise. As a member of the police, he was not used to such acceptance from her social class. He had lost his sense of where Melisande was in the crowd, but he knew precisely where Barclay was standing, only yards away, looking at him with distaste. How long would it be before he told Mrs. Costain that Runcorn was a policeman?

But Barclay was not actually looking at Runcorn, he was staring at the girl in green, his eyes so intent on her face that Runcorn knew she must be aware of it, even uncomfortable. There was a brooding emotion in Barclay that seemed a mixture of longing and anger, and when the man with auburn hair who had also watched her approached, his face tight and bitter, for an instant the tension between her and Barclay was so palpable that others were momentarily uncomfortable as well.

"Morning, Newbridge," Barclay's voice was curt.

"Morning, Barclay," Newbridge replied. "Pleasant weather."

Everyone else was silent.

"I doubt it will last," Barclay responded.

"Do you imagine we will have a white Christmas?" Reverend Costain put in quickly. "It is in little over a week now. It would be nice for our party."

Barclay's eyebrows rose. "White?" he said sarcastically, as if the word held a dozen other, more pungent meanings. "Hardly."

The girl in green glanced over at him with amusement and then a sudden little shiver, hunching her shoulders as though she were cold, although she was well dressed and there was no wind.

"Olivia?" Costain said anxiously, as if to distract her. "Come meet our visitor, Mr. Runcorn. Mr. Runcorn, my sister, Miss Olivia Costain."

"Don't fuss," his wife's voice was soft. Had Runcorn not been standing so close he would not have heard her.

The vicar was visibly disconcerted. He looked from Barclay to Olivia and clearly did not know how to address the deeper meaning that was understood between them. The attempted introduction was lost in the tension between them.

Barclay nodded curtly and walked over towards Melisande, who was waiting for him on the path by the lych-gate. Runcorn watched him go, and then for a moment his eyes met Melisande's and he was unaware of anyone else. Newbridge brushed past him, breaking the moment. He reached Olivia and said something to her. She replied, her voice cool and light. Her words were courteous, her face almost empty of expression. Then she turned and walked away. Runcorn was certain in that instant that she disliked Newbridge.

He thanked Mrs. Costain for her kindness, glanced briefly at the others in acknowledgment, then excused himself. He made his way across the graveyard between the headstones, the carved angels, and the funeral urns and into the shadow of the yew trees beyond. He walked out of the farther gate into the road, his mind still whirling.

It was his profession to watch people and read reactions. There was so much more to investigating than attending to the words given in an answer. It was as much the way these words were said, the hesitations, the angle of the head, the movement and the stillness that told him of the passions beneath. That small group in the churchyard had been torn by emotions too powerful to control except with intense effort. The air was heavy, tingling on the skin like that before the breaking of a storm.

In spite of his separateness, his observation of it so intellectually cool, he was as much a victim as any of them. He was just as human, as vulnerable and every bit as absurd. What could be more ridiculous than the way he felt about Melisande, a woman to whom he could never be more than a public servant that she had been able to assist, because she had had the courage to do the right thing in spite of her brother's disapproval?

He went back to Mrs. Owen's house because he knew she had cooked Sunday dinner for him and it would be a graceless thing not to return and eat it, despite already feeling as if the comfortable walls of the house would close him in almost unbearably. And the last thing he wanted was trivial conversation, no matter how well meant. But he was a man of habit, and he had learned the cost of bad manners.

At least he had an excuse to leave quickly. The weather being exceptionally pleasant for December, he was determined to walk as far as he could and still return by dusk. The wild, lonely paths along the shore with the turbulent noise of breaking water and screaming gulls fit his mood perfectly. It was nature eternal and far beyond man's control. It was an escape to become part of it, simply by hearing the sounds, feeling the wind in his face, and looking at the limitless horizon. It was big and impersonal, and that comforted him. He saw in it a kind of truth.

*T*he next day Runcorn walked the shore all the way from Beaumaris north and east to Penmon Point. He stood and stared at the lighthouse and Puffin Island beyond. The day after he went in the other direction, all the way past the Menai Bridge until he could see the great towers of Caernarfon Castle on the opposite shore, beneath the vast, white-crowned peaks of Snowdonia. The following day he walked aimlessly in the hills above Beaumaris until he was exhausted.

Even so, he did not sleep well. He rose at seven, shaved and dressed, and went outside into the winter dawn. The air had a hard edge of ice on it, so sharp he gasped as he breathed it in. But he found a perverse pleasure in it, also. It was clean and bitter, and he imagined he could see the distances it had blown across, the dark, glimmering water and the starlight. Eight days to go. Perhaps they would have a white Christmas after all.

Without realizing it he had walked uphill towards the church again. Its tower loomed massive against the lightening sky. He went in through the lych-gate and up the path, then around through the grave-yard, picking his way across the grass crisp with frost. The dawn was sending pale shafts of light up in the east and throwing shadows from the grave-stones and the occasional marble angel.

Perhaps that was why he was almost upon the body before he realized what it was. She was lying at the base of a carved cross, her white gown frozen hard, her face stiff, her black hair spread out in a cloud around her like a shadow. The only color was the blood drenching the lower half of her body, which flooded scarlet with the strengthening daylight.

Runcorn was too horrified to move. He stood star-ing at her as if he had seen an apparition, and if he waited, his vision would clear and it would vanish. But the cold moved into his bones, the fingers of light crept further around her body, and she remained as terribly real. He knew who she was, Olivia Costain, the girl in green who had walked up the aisle of the church as if on a grassy lea.

He moved at last, going forward to bend onto one knee and touch her freezing hand. It was more than cold, the fingers clenched and locked in place. Her eyes were wide open. Even here, like this, something of her beauty remained, a delicacy to the bones, which wrenched inside him with pity for what she had been.

He looked down at the terrible wound in her stomach, clotted with thick blood, the flesh itself hidden. She must have been standing close to the grave, with her back to the cross, facing whoever it was that had done this to her. She had not been running away. He studied the ground and saw no damage to the grass except what he himself had done, bending over her. There was nothing to say she had fought, no marks on either of her hands, or on her arms or throat. Her killer could not have taken her by surprise from behind, they had stood face-to-face. The attack must have been sudden and terrible.

From such an injury she would have bled to death

very quickly, he hoped in just moments. It was bright, arterial blood, the force of life. Surely it would not be possible to stand close enough to someone and inflict such a blow without being stained by blood oneself?

He stepped back and automatically cast his eyes about for the weapon. He did not expect to find it, but he must be certain. He could see nothing, no trace of red in the white daylight, no irregularity in the frost-pale grass, except the way he himself had come, as both she and her killer must have also, before the dew was iced hard.

People would pass this way soon. He must find someone to watch the body, keep anyone else from disturbing it. He must report it to the local police. At the very least he must prevent Costain from seeing her himself.

Who'd be closest? The sexton. But where to find him? He turned slowly, seeking a well-worn path, another gate. There was nothing. He went a few steps to the east, but there was nothing but more graves. Increasing his pace, he went in the opposite direction, around the corner of the church tower, and saw a more trodden way and a path at the end. Running now and slipping a little, he turned to the wall and the small cottage beyond nestled in its apple orchard. He banged on the back door.

It was answered by an elderly man, clearly in the middle of his breakfast.

"Are you the sexton, sir?" Runcorn asked.

"I am. Can I help you?"

Runcorn told him the harsh facts and asked him to stand guard over the body, then he followed the man's directions to the cottage of Constable Warner, who would still be at home at this hour.

Warner was just finishing his breakfast and his wife was reluctant to disturb him until she saw Runcorn's face in the inside light, and the shock in his eyes. Then she made no demur. She passed him a cup of tea, and insisted he drink it while he explained his profession and his errand to Warner himself, a large, soft-spoken man in his early forties.

"I suppose you'll be used to this, coming from London, an' all," he said a little huskily, after Runcorn had described the scene to him, and the little he had deduced from it. "I never dealt with murder before, 'cepting as you'd call a fight that ended badly mur-der." His face was filled not only with sorrow but with a kind of helplessness as the enormity of his own task dawned on him. Runcorn could see his fear.

"If I can help," he offered, and immediately won-dered if he had trespassed already, implying how-ever obliquely, that the local force was inferior. He regretted it, but it was too late.

Warner swallowed. "Well, we'll be getting some-one from the mainland, no doubt," he said quickly. "Maybe the chief constable, or such. But I'd be mighty grateful if you'd lend a hand until then, see-ing as you have the experience."

"Of course," Runcorn agreed. "First thing, some-one'll have to tell her family, and as soon as possible, get a doctor to look at her. Then we should have her put somewhere decent."

"Yes." Warner looked bewildered. "Yes, I'll do that. Poor vicar." He pushed his hand up over his brow, blinking rapidly. "What a terrible thing to happen." He glanced at Runcorn hopefully. "I suppose it couldn't be an accident of some kind? Could she have . . . fell, somehow?"

29

"No," Runcorn said simply. He did not bother to go over the details again, or even mention the absurdity of Olivia Costain walking alone at night in the graveyard carrying a knife large enough to cause an injury like the one he had seen. She had not tripped, she had fallen backwards from the weight of the assault. The blade had not been found.

Warner sighed, his face pale but flushed unnaturally across the cheeks, his eyes downcast. "Sorry, I just . . ." He looked up again suddenly. "We aren't used to this kind o' thing here. Known Miss Olivia since she were . . . little. Who'd do this to her?"

"We have to find that out," Runcorn said simply. "It's where our duty gets hard and ugly, and it matters we do it right."

Warner rose to his feet, scraping the kitchen chair on the floor as he pushed it back. "I'll go an' tell the vicar, an' Mrs. Costain. She'll be torn to bits. They were very close, she an' Miss Olivia, more like real sisters they were, not just in-law, like. Will you . . . will you go and find Dr. Trimby? His house is hard to find, my wife'll take you. Then I'd better get a message to the inspector in Bangor, and no doubt he'll be sending for Sir Alan Faraday from Caernarfon."

Runcorn accepted without further discussion. A few moments later he was walking beside Mrs. Warner as she led him through a hasty shortcut across the road and through one back street after another until they arrived at the door of Dr. Trimby's house. It was now nearly nine o'clock on a gusty morning, the streets were busy, and there were three or four people already waiting in his surgery.

Trimby's name did not suit him. He was short and stocky with flyaway hair, a shirt that defied the iron, and a cravat as unfashionable as it was possible to be. Nothing of his apparel matched anything else. However, his attention was instant and complete. Once Mrs. Warner had told him who Runcorn was, he listened with a mixture of grief and total concentration. He made no notes at all, but Runcorn had no doubt that he remembered every detail. His blunt, asymmetrical face was heavy with sadness.

"I suppose you'd better take me to her," he said, hauling himself to his feet. On the way out he picked up his bag, good leather once, but now bearing the scars of twenty years of service in all weathers.

They walked back up to the graveyard more or less the way Runcorn had come with Mrs. Warner, and found the sexton still standing guard alone and shivering with cold.

Trimby looked past him at the body and his face bleached so pale Runcorn was afraid for a moment that he was going to collapse. But after a painfully intense effort, he regained his composure, then bent and began to make his professional examination.

Runcorn excused the sexton and waited quietly in the rising wind, growing colder and colder as the minutes passed.

Finally Trimby stood up awkwardly, his legs stiff from kneeling, his balance a little uncertain.

"No later than midnight," he said hoarsely. He coughed and began again. "Far as I can tell from the rigor mortis. But you can see that yourself with the frost, I expect. Cold, exposure makes a difference. Look for whoever saw her last, if you can trust them. Can't . . . can't make a wound like that without getting blood on yourself. She didn't fight." His voice broke and he took a long, difficult moment to regain his self-control. "Nothing much else I can tell you. Can't learn anything more from this. I'll get her out of here, get her . . . decent." He turned to go.

"Doctor . . ." Runcorn called out.

Trimby waved a hand at him impatiently. "You can see as much as I can. This is your business, not mine." He continued to walk rapidly between the gravestones.

Runcorn's legs were longer and he caught up with him. "It's not all you can tell me," he said, matching his step to Trimby's. "You know her, tell me something about her. Who would have done this?"

"A raving madman!" Trimby snapped back without turning to look at him or slacken his pace.

Runcorn snatched his arm and pulled him up short, swinging him around a little. It was a thing he had never done before in all the violent and tragic cases he had ever dealt with. His own emotions were more deeply wrenched than he had imagined. "No, it was not a madman," he said savagely. "It was someone she knew and was not afraid of. You know that as well as I do. She was facing him, she wasn't run-

33

ning away, and she didn't fight back because she wasn't expecting him to strike her. Why was she here anyway? Who would she meet in a graveyard alone, late at night?"

Trimby stared at him, angry and defensive. "What kind of world do you live in where a man who would do that to a woman is considered sane?" he asked, his voice trembling.

Runcorn saw the profound emotion in him, the bewilderment and the sense of loss far deeper than what he must have felt from the expected deaths he encountered in his practice from time to time. Olivia had presumably been his patient and he might have known her all her life. Runcorn answered honestly. "When we say 'madman,' we mean someone unknown to us, who acts without reason, attacking at random, someone outside the world we understand. This wasn't someone like that, and I think you know it."

Trimby lowered his gaze. "If there were anything I could tell you, I would," he replied. "I have no idea who it was, or why this happened. That is your job to find out, God help you." And he turned and strode away through the last of the gravestones, leaving Runcorn alone, cold, and spattered by the first heavy drops of rain.

*I*t was a miserable day of small duties before Runcorn finally met again with Constable Warner and told him what Trimby had said. The medical evidence, such as it was, confirmed his own deduction, but added nothing that was of help. Olivia Costain had been stabbed in the stomach with a broad blade. The single thrust had severed the artery and she had bled to death within moments, falling backwards from where she had been standing. As Runcorn had supposed, there were no defensive wounds on her hands or arms, or anywhere else on her body.

"She probably died before midnight," he finished.

Warner looked tired, his eyes red-rimmed as if he had been sleepless far longer than one interminable day. They sat at the same kitchen table as they had in the morning, again with a pot of tea between them.

"I told the vicar," he said miserably. "Poor man was shattered. I think Mrs. Costain took it even harder. Very close, they were."

"Did you find out who was the last to see Miss Costain alone?" Runcorn asked, bringing him back to the facts. He had seen constables profoundly shaken by death before. The first few times were the hardest, especially when the victim was particularly vulnerable, young, old, or in some other way helpless. It helped to concentrate on the little they could do now that was of use.

Warner looked up. "Oh. Yes. Housekeeper saw her leave at about ten, or a few minutes after. Said she was just going for a walk. Seems she did that quite often, walked alone, even after dark. Didn't go far."

"So there are two hours during which she could have been killed?"

"Yes, seems like it," Warner agreed. "I asked everyone where they were. Not a lot of help. The vicar was in his study, Mrs. Costain was in the library reading until she went to bed at about eleven. Their neighbors in the big house up the road would be Mr. John Barclay and his sister, Mrs. Ewart, widow so they say. He went out to visit a friend, but he walked home alone and didn't disturb the servants when he got in. So there's no proof where he was after about half past ten. She was in bed, but she dismissed her maid, so we've only her word." Warner looked more and more unhappy. "And the curate, Kelsall, lives alone in a little cottage half a mile away. Mr. Newbridge, who had been courting Miss Olivia until recently, lives about two miles away, and he was working in his study until eleven. But he dismissed his manservant after dinner, so we have only his word also."

"Reasonable," Runcorn admitted reluctantly. "I couldn't account for myself either. A late walk on a clear winter evening is a natural thing to do. Have a look at the stars. You can really see them here. And most people who have servants let them go if there's no need to keep them up. Anybody see her after that? See anybody about, or hear anything? What about servants, courting maybe? Any neighbors up?"

Warner shook his head. "Asked anywhere I knew of, Mr. Runcorn, and not a thing I can see as helps us at all. All the other neighbors so far can say where they were, 'cos they all have families, or servants as saw them. Not that they all knew Miss Olivia that well, except in passing, as it were. Terribly shaken up, they were. We've never had anything like that here. It's . . ." he stopped, lost for words.

He shook his head slowly, avoiding Runcorn's eyes. "Got a message, chief constable's going to be here sometime late tomorrow. He'll take over then. Can't say as I'm sorry. This is not the kind of thing I know how to handle, Mr. Runcorn. The odd robbery now and then, even a barn burning or a real bad fight I can deal with, but this is different. Got everybody frightened, and sick with grief, it has. Glad enough to have Sir Alan take charge of it. But I'm obliged to you for your help. We'll hand over a tidy investigation, evidence all straight and done right, thanks to you." He smiled very slightly, his shoulders easing a little, his color ashen as if at last he could let go of some of the burden which he had carried today. Only yesterday he could not have even thought of it in his worst nightmare. "I'm sure Sir Alan would want to thank you himself, but for us here, I'm grateful, Mr. Runcorn."

Runcorn knew it would be this way, he had no jurisdiction in Anglesey, no standing beyond that of any other responsible citizen. And yet he felt absurdly disappointed. It was not that he wanted work. The case was tragic, nothing about it was obvious, and he certainly had no idea who could have done it, or why. But he wanted to see it to the end, he wanted to find out who had destroyed a young woman who had been uniquely alive and full of grace. And perhaps also he had wanted to be of value, here so very close to Melisande, not merely another onlooker. Dealing with violence and fear was the one thing he was good at. It was where his skills were truly valued.

But of course the chief constable was coming. It was too grave a case for him not to. It was not even twenty-four hours since the murder, and panic was already rising, fear cold and dark, wakening like the wind rattling at the windows. Except that the wind could be shut out, and fear entered in spite of all the locks and bars in the world.

"Glad to help," he said quietly. "Sorry it wasn't more."

Warner held out his hand suddenly. "Very glad you were here, Mr. Runcorn. Very glad."

Runcorn took it. There did not seem any more to add, and now he would leave to be alone, to face the fact that he did not belong here as he walked down the incline towards Mrs. Owen's house, and another night before an empty day.

*B*ut in spite of his resolution, by early evening Runcorn walked back towards Warner's house, past the field where the redwings were still busy. He was hungry for information, though he knew it was foolish because they could not tell him anything. It was no longer his concern, he was not one of them. The reminder was painful. It forced him to realize more vividly an emptiness inside himself, a growing need for something more than he had.

As he passed the entrance to the churchyard, memory and grief clenched inside him again, making him even colder. He was surprised to see John Barclay ahead of him, walking beside a man almost his own height, a man who was bare-headed even in this wind, his hair thick and fair. He had an almost military precision to his step, and even at a distance Runcorn could see the elegance in the cut of his clothes. It had to be Sir Alan Faraday, the chief constable. But why was he talking so closely to Barclay, as if they were friends?

Runcorn stopped, and perhaps the unexpected action caught Barclay's eye, because he put his hand on Faraday's arm and said something, and both of them turned towards Runcorn. Barclay took the first step forward, and there was something obscurely threatening to his action.

Runcorn stood his ground.

"Good evening," Barclay said quite loudly, speaking when they were still several yards distant. "Runcorn, isn't it?"

"Good evening, Mr. Barclay," Runcorn replied, still not moving.

Closer to, the other man was good looking, his eyes were steady and remarkably blue.

"This is the London fellow I was mentioning," Barclay told him. "Runcorn gave us a hand before you could get here." He looked at Runcorn. "Sir Alan Faraday, chief constable of the county. Obviously this is in his hands now. Very serious case, indeed. Warrants the highest attention, I think, before the horror of it can cause public fear and unrest. But we're obliged to you for your help in the beginning."

"Indeed," Faraday affirmed, watching cautiously. "Very good of you to step in so professionally. It seems you've left all the evidence well ordered for us. Very nasty case, and of course people are terrified. It looks as if we have a lunatic on the island. We must do all we can to reassure them, and see that panic does not take hold."

Runcorn was at a loss to know how to respond graciously and without allowing his emotions to betray him. It was at times like this he wished desperately that he had more polish, more of the assurance of a gentleman, which would allow him to assume he was in the right and demand others to assume it also. Instead, he felt like a good servant being dismissed for the night. And yet to resent it would make him look absurd.

But he was absurd. It stung, it was humiliating.

Monk would have known how to carry it off with such flare that Faraday and Barclay would have been the ones to feel foolish. But he was not Monk, he was not clever with words. Above all, he had no grace, no elegance.

"You are welcome to such help as I can give, Sir Alan," he replied instead, and heard himself sound as if he were indeed a servant asking for approval.

Faraday nodded. "Good of you," he said briefly. "We should be able to find the fellow soon enough. Small place, and all that. Decent people. Terrible tragedy, just before Christmas."

Barclay looked at Faraday. "I'd like a word with Runcorn, if you don't mind. I'll meet you up at the vicarage in a moment or two."

The chief constable acknowledged Runcorn with a brief nod, and within moments he was fifty yards away, walking easily as if miles would have meant little to him.

"Good man," Barclay observed with satisfaction. "Ex-army, of course. He'll sort this out, calm people's fears, and get us back to something like normal. Can't undo the memory or the loss, but no one could do that. You can't help any more, Runcorn. These are not your people, not the class you are used to dealing with. I'm sure you mean well, but you won't understand them, or their ways."

Runcorn wished to say something, but everything that came to his mind sounded to him as if he were trying to defend himself. He remained standing silently in the wind, the grief of the churchyard, the reality of death and loss overwhelming. He should not give even a passing thought to his own feelings.

"As long as you find who killed Miss Costain, it hardly matters who assists you," he retaliated.

"My dear fellow, of course it matters!" Barclay said hotly, but with a continued smile on his face, more of a pulling back of the lips to show perfect teeth. "We cannot help the dead, but the feelings of the living matter very much. Our conduct can make an enormous difference to their fear, their sense of danger and disorder. But what I really wanted to say to you, privately from Faraday, is that he is an excellent man, and very soon to become engaged to marry my sister, Mrs. Ewart, who as you may recall is widowed." His eyes did not waver from Runcorn's face. "It is a most fortunate match and will offer her everything she wishes. I hope I do not have to spell out in detail how unfortunate it would be if you were to mention your past professional involvement in London, however innocently intended. It can only raise questions and require explanations that would be wiser to leave unsaid. So please do not force yourself to anyone's attention by making apparent that you have a past acquaintance, however superficial."

Runcorn felt as if he had been slapped so hard the breath was momentarily knocked out of him. He drew in his breath, and found nothing to say in return, not a word that could touch the wound in him.

"I knew you'd understand," Barclay said blithely. "Hope this wretched matter is all ended rather faster than you dealt with the other business. What a mess! Still, this seems clearer. I'm obliged to you. Good day." And without waiting for Runcorn to think of a reply, he turned and followed after Faraday.

 he next two days passed in a chaotic unhappiness as Faraday took over all that Runcorn had left, of course with the help of Warner, who had no choice in such matters. Warner's position reminded Runcorn a bit of his own when Monk had been in the Metropolitan Police with him, years ago. Monk was always cleverer, always so sure of himself, at least on the surface. Runcorn had not known then of the private ghosts and demons that haunted him, for his own blindness had seen nothing but the iron-hard grace of the mask with which Monk protected himself. But if Faraday had anything of Monk's complexity, Runcorn found no trace of it in his smooth face, no vulnerability in the eyes, no leap of the mind to understand more passionately than others.

Runcorn would have been glad if at least Faraday had had Monk's skill. More than any personal rivalry, it mattered that they find who killed Olivia Costain. And he realized with a rising sickness in his stomach, they must also prevent the murderer from killing anyone else who might threaten him in any way. Runcorn's mind turned immediately to another unique and lovely woman—Melisande. That was the core of his fear, and for that he would sacrifice any dignity or personal pride, any ambition whatever.

But two days went by, and as far as he could tell, or hear from a fearful Mrs. Owen, no progress at all had been made. It was now less than a week until Christmas. Parties were canceled. Whenever they could, people remained in their homes. After dark the streets were deserted, even though there was no snow yet, and the wind no fiercer or colder than before. There were whispers of madness, even of something loose that was less than human, some creature of the dark that must be destroyed before the light of Christmas and hope returned to the world.

In the street a little before noon, Runcorn passed Trimby, still looking as untidy as before. He was striding out, his coattails flying, his hat abandoned and his hair streaming out like a wind-blown banner, and he went by without speaking, consumed in his own thoughts.

Runcorn could bear it no longer. He went to the vicarage where he knew Faraday would be, and found him speaking to writers and journalists from the island, and from mainland Wales as far away as Denbigh and Harlech.

No one took any notice as one more man pushed his way into the crowded withdrawing room, and he stood at the back and listened while Faraday did his best to dispel the fear rising with every new question. What kind of a lunatic was loose among them? Had there been sightings? When? Where? By whom? Could somebody be sheltering this creature? Did the vicar have any opinions? Why had Olivia Costain been the victim?

Faraday kept on trying to soothe the fear. At the end, he answered so decisively that Olivia was an exemplary young woman, known and loved in the community and of an unblemished reputation, that his very vehemence suggested doubt.

And when Runcorn spoke to him later, alone, his words reinforced that impression. They were in the room Costain had set apart for Faraday's use, a cozy study with a good fire burning, and walls crowded with books and hung with an odd jumble of paintings, cartoons, and drawings. There were papers spread over the table and a pen and inkwell beside them.

"Thank you for coming," Faraday said rather abruptly. "As long as you're here, I might as well ask if you have anything to add. You seem to have interested yourself rather much." It was a graceless turn of phrase, but he was asking for help.

"It wasn't a madman," Runcorn said grimly. "You know that, sir. The evidence says it was someone she knew." He remained standing, too angry to sit, although in truth, he had not been invited to do so.

"No," Faraday agreed unhappily. "At least, I appreciate that she knew him, but I think it's not wise to say so." He looked up at Runcorn intently. "I hope you will have the decency not to speak irresponsibly? It will only increase the fear there is already. As long as people think it is someone they don't know, at least they are not turning upon each other." He seemed to be concerned that Runcorn understood. "There is a sense of unity, a willingness to help. That is why I am not saying that she was a difficult young woman with some very unsatisfactory ideas, even dangerous in a way. Poor Costain had his troubles with her. She appeared to be unwilling to settle down. She refused several very good offers of marriage, and it looked as if she was not prepared to become adult and accept her role in society. She expected her brother to keep her indefinitely, while she drifted from one rather foolish dream to another. Her virtue had not yet been questioned openly, but it was only a matter of time before that happened, which is hard for any man, but especially one in his profession."

Thoughts raged through Runcorn's mind, memories of Olivia walking up the aisle of the church with the same careless grace she might have displayed on the beach, the foam breaking around her, the wind off the sea in her face. Why should she marry to suit her brother's social or religious life? Then Runcorn realized he was actually thinking of Melisande marrying Faraday to suit Barclay's ambition, and to free him from responsibility for her.

He looked at Faraday, straight-backed, good-looking, unimaginative, comfortable. Did he love Melisande? Did he adore her, see in her unique courage

and grace? Certainly she possessed a will strong
enough to defy convention and risk her own safety
to give witness to a crime, as she had done in London for Monk and Runcorn when they had been
pursuing a dangerous assassin. Did Faraday care
desperately that she was happy, that nothing in her
was forced, crushed, distorted into duty rather than
belief? Or was she just a lovely and very suitable
wife, one of whom he need never be anxious or
ashamed, one who would fit all his social and politi-
cal ambitions?

That was what Barclay wanted for her, never to
be in want or need in the conventional sense, to be
respected, even envied, to be secure for the rest of
her life. In many ways perhaps that was more than
most women could expect. And yet Runcorn, who
could offer her nothing but admiration, was incensed
for her. He wanted her to have so much more than
that.

It was impertinent of him, and arrogant. Perhaps
she was realistic, and for her such a marriage would
be sufficient.

He finished the rest of his conversation with

Faraday hardly knowing what he was saying, except that at the end he was dismissed knowing little more than he had when he came in. There was fear and confusion everywhere, and Faraday was, so far, at a loss to know where to proceed next. His knowledge of men and events, his ability to command, did not extend to anything like this.

*T*he following morning, Runcorn set off alone. He followed the south shore of the island, over rocks and sand, always watching the tide, aware of its danger. The sea was both provider and destroyer, it granted no mercy to anyone. He had read that somewhere. Looking at its constantly shifting surface, its blind power, its beauty and deceit, he believed that absolutely.

He walked until he could see the towers of Caernarfon across the strait, then he rested a short while and walked back again through occasional rain, with the wind behind him. He was exhausted and it was late in the day when, without thought, his feet took him back to walk up towards the churchyard. He knew why, Barclay and Melisande were staying in the big house beyond the green. If there was anywhere he might catch a glimpse of her, it was here.

It was a quarter of an hour later as he was watching the light fade on the hills that he heard her voice behind him. Her footsteps had been soundless on the grass.

"Mr. Runcorn?"

He swung around, his breath catching in his throat. He had difficulty answering her. She was wearing a dark gown with a hooded cloak over it to protect her against the wind. The amber light from the last of the sun was soft on her face, accentuating her cheekbones and the line of her chin. He had never seen anyone so beautiful, or so able to hope, to care, and to be hurt.

"Good evening, Mrs. Ewart," he said hoarsely.

"I am glad you are here," she answered. "Sir Alan is a good man, and I suppose John was right to send for him . . ." she hesitated. "But I don't believe he has the experience of . . . of a terrible crime like this, to be able to learn quickly enough what happened, and who is responsible."

Should he try to comfort her? He could see the fear in her eyes. She was right, Faraday had no idea how to investigate a murder. It was not really what chief constables were for. He was doing it because Melisande was here, and perhaps because the crime had raised such terror on the island that people were close to panic. The brutality of it was something they had never experienced before.

Should Runcorn lie to her, he wondered.

"Quickly enough?" he questioned. "Do you fear it will happen again?" Why had he asked her that? It was no comfort at all.

"Won't it?" she said softly. "You know about these things. Does somebody do this once and then stop? Won't they defend themselves if we get close to them, if we seem to be about to tear the mask off and show who they really are?"

He shivered in spite of himself. Her fear touched him more sharply than the dusk wind. She was right, the only safety lay in swiftness, in striking be-fore the victim knew the direction of the blow, and striking fatally. He longed to be able to protect her, but he had no duty, no place here at all.

"Won't they?" she repeated. "Have I put you in an impossible position?" She looked away from him. "I am very afraid that we are out of our depth. Sir Alan is speaking as if it is some random beast come out of the wild places in the center of the island, the hills beyond our climbing." She stopped abruptly, biting her lower lip, afraid to say the rest of what was crowding her mind.

He said it for her. "But you think the beast comes from within someone here in the houses and streets you think you know?"

Her eyes opened wide and there was a warmth in them, even a kind of relief. "Don't you? Please be honest with me, Mr. Runcorn. This is too terrible for us to be exchanging lies because we think they are easier. Olivia deserves better than that, and for our own sakes we can't afford to keep looking the other way."

Why did she think so? She had not seen the body as he had. What had she heard or felt that she understood this? Who was she afraid for? Did she know who it was, or perhaps suspect? She knew Costain and his wife, and of course she knew her brother Barclay. She had been fond of Olivia, so it was possible she had learned from her something of Newbridge, or even of the curate Kelsall. Was she afraid the investigation would expose things that were ugly in any of them, or all?

Everyone has actions, wounds they are ashamed of, secrets they will fight to protect. Someone might even lash out to protect the memory of Olivia herself. Grief can cause many violent things no one could foresee, even in those most affected. Sometimes it deepens love, other times it breaks it.

"Have you told Sir Alan your fears?" He hated even mentioning the man's name.

She shook her head fractionally. "No. I think he has enough to worry about, with the feeling that's growing among people, and their demands for help, and for a solution. Nobody can just . . . produce it because it's needed. We are not children to have all our fears soothed away. Something terrible has happened, and Alan cannot undo it for us, or provide the answers we want." Distress, and something like pity, touched her face. "I don't suppose anyone can."

Runcorn wondered if she meant only what she said—that they must all endure it because there was no other way, and it was unfair to expect it. Was she defending Faraday, or saying he could not handle the task, or both? Runcorn struggled to read her eyes, the line of her lips, but it was too dark to see clearly anymore, and he did not understand anyway.

He knew she was afraid, but then only a fool would not be. Whatever the truth was, it would bring pain. Their lives would never heal over the things they would hear of each other, the shortcomings, the secrets ordinary life could have left decently covered. Murder swept all that away.

Did she love Faraday? The helplessness and the mercy of it was that one did not have to be perfect to be loved, one did not even have to be especially good. Love was a gift, a grace. He had never tested it himself. He was clumsy, ungenerous, never knowing how to respond.

He longed now to say something that would comfort her, be of more help in the days ahead, which would hold pain for her, but all he could do was tell her the truth. Of course he wanted to protect her, most of all from the actual danger. It was the one skill he had, but he was unable to use it because this was not his jurisdiction. He had no more authority here than the postman or the fishmonger—less, because he did not belong.

"Mr. Runcorn . . ." she said tentatively.

"Yes?"

"You found Olivia's body, didn't you." It was not really a question. She was leading to something further.

"Yes." The misery of it was in his voice.

"Do you think she was killed by a madman, someone none of us know?"

He hesitated.

"Please?" she said urgently. "This is no time for comfortable lies. Do not treat me as if I were foolish. Olivia was my friend. I really cared for her very much, even though I knew her well only a short time. We . . . we had much in common.

"I would like to know the truth, and Alan will not tell me."

"Then . . ." he started, and stopped. She was inviting him to tell her something that the man she was going to marry had refused her.

"Your silence is answer." She turned away from him, her voice tight with disappointment.

He could not bear it. "No, it was someone she knew," he admitted. "She was facing him, not running away."

She looked at him again, her expression filled with grief. "Poor Olivia. Can you think of anything more terrible? I want to ask you if she felt much pain, but I am not sure if I can endure the answer."

"No," he said quickly. "It can only have been a few moments at most."

"Thank you." Her voice was soft. "I'm sorry to have . . . Mr. Runcorn, will you please help us? I don't think we know how to deal with this. We are not used to such . . . discomfort of the mind, such feelings of pain and fear when we don't know what to do."

He was stunned, and yet this was exactly what he

had wanted, to help! Had she any idea what she asked of him? He had no authority, no rights here at all. Faraday would resent it. Barclay would be furious. He should tell her that, explain all the reasons why he could not do it. Instead, he simply said, "Yes, of course I will."

"Thank you." The faintest smile softened her mouth for a moment. "I am very grateful. I should not have kept you standing here in the cold so long. Good night, Mr. Runcorn." And slowly, with intense grace, she turned and walked away.

He was too overwhelmed to reply. He remained where he was, shivering in the wind until he could no longer see her figure in the shadows, then at last he turned to go back to Mrs. Owen.

There was only one obvious place to begin, and that was with Constable Warner.

Runcorn arrived at Warner's kitchen the next morning at eight o'clock, having risen when it was still dark and walked up the incline so as to know exactly when Warner turned his light on.

"Doing everything we can think of," Warner said, offering Runcorn fresh, hot tea, which was accepted gratefully. The day was bitter, a raw wind edged with sleet blowing in from the east. "Hard to know what to do next," he went on, bending to open up the stove so the heat spread out into the room. He did not look at Runcorn. "Porridge?" he asked.

"Thank you." It had been too early to expect breakfast from Mrs. Owen, and actually he had barely thought of it.

"I feel helpless," Warner added, his voice full of misery.

Runcorn recognized it as an oblique way of telling him that Faraday was making no progress, and possibly had little idea what to do next. He had painted himself into something of a corner with his assumption that it was a madman. It was easy enough to understand why he had done so, faced with the brutality of the crime and the horror it had awoken in everyone, family and stranger alike. The whole town suffered under a weight of shock as if life had been darkened for all of them. Something irreparable had been destroyed.

Warner was too loyal to say outright that Faraday was floundering; in fact, he would not even look Runcorn in the eye as he tried to find the right words, but that was what he meant.

"He's going to have to acknowledge that it was someone she knew," Warner said aloud. "Nobody'll want to think so, but you can't get away from it." He stirred the porridge a final time. "Then you can start asking the questions that'll lead us to the truth." His voice carried more confidence than he must have felt.

Warner ladled the porridge into two bowls and brought it to the table, along with milk and spoons and both salt and sugar. "But what kind of questions?" He faced Runcorn fully now, the awkwardness of pretending he was not really looking for help had been negotiated.

They both started to eat while Runcorn thought carefully of how to reply. The porridge was thick and smooth and the more he ate, the more he liked it. He wondered what he could say that was honest and still kept a remnant of tact? Or did tact matter any more at this point? Surely now it was harsh and dangerous enough that only the truth would serve? If he were taking over this case from someone else, what would he do, were he able to have complete control of it?

Warner was waiting for him to speak, his face pale with the deep exhaustion of fear.

"I'd be plain," Runcorn told him quietly. "There's not a lot of use going back over where everyone was because they've already said, and no one's going to admit to a lie. I suppose you haven't found the blade?"

Warner shook his head.

"It would have come from someone's kitchen," Runcorn observed.

"We could see who's missing one?" Warner suggested doubtfully. "But that'd mean pretty well saying as we thought it was one of them, or we couldn't even look."

"And for all we know, it could've been washed and put back," Runcorn added.

Warner winced, his face clearly mirroring his racing imagination, the Sunday joint carved with the weapon of murder.

Runcorn clenched his teeth. This was difficult, but he had promised Melisande that he would help, which meant that he must do so, wherever the truth led him, even to angering Faraday and possibly making an enemy of him. Nobody would welcome the sort of questions that must be asked, but to investigate other than honestly would serve no purpose. However painful the truth of why Olivia had been killed, and by whom, it must be found. And, inevitably, other secrets, follies, and shames would also be uncovered. Perhaps even Melisande would be forced to see things she might have preferred to overlook. Runcorn had a strong feeling that very little would be the same afterwards.

Should he have warned her of his prediction? Should he do so now? Of course he knew the answer in his heart. In the past he had sometimes done what was expedient, said the right things, turned the occasional blind eye. It had won him the promotion Monk had never received. It had also earned him Monk's contempt, and if he were honest, his own as well. He could never have Melisande's love—it hurt to say so—but he would keep the integrity which made him able to look at her without shame.

"I don't know whether Sir Alan will look into the weapon more closely or not," he finally said to Warner. "But what I would do, were it with me, is to learn more about Miss Costain herself, until I knew everything I could about who really loved her, hated her. Who might have seen her as a threat, or a rival? And to do that I would also have to learn a lot more about her family and all those others who were part of her life."

"I see," Warner said slowly, thinking about what that could mean. He searched Runcorn's face, and saw there was no pretense in it, and no way of evading the truth. "Then that's what we'll have to do, isn't it." It was a statement. "I've only dealt with robberies before, and a little bit of embezzlement, a fire once. It was ugly. I expect this is going to be far worse. We'll need your help, Mr. Runcorn." This time there was a lift of doubt in his voice. He was asking as openly as he dared to.

For Runcorn the die was already cast, he had

promised Melisande. Warner could add nothing to that. But he realized now that to investigate with any honesty he would have to go to Faraday and ask for his permission, which the chief constable had every right to refuse. Even the thought of facing him, pleading to be allowed to have a part in the case, clenched his stomach like a cramp. But as an investigator he would be useless without Faraday's approval. The simplest solution might be to ask and be refused. Melisande would have to accept that. She would see Faraday's inadequacy and recognize it for the pride it was, and excuse Runcorn.

But would he excuse himself? Not even for an instant. Part of honesty would be using his skill to ask Faraday in such a way that he could not refuse. He had made enough mistakes in the past with clumsiness of words, lack of judgment, selfishness, that he ought to have learned all the lessons by now. If he wanted to badly enough, he could place Faraday in a position where it would be impossible for him to refuse help. This was his one chance to become the man he had always failed to be. He had let pride, anger, and ambition stop him.

"I'll have to have Sir Alan's permission," he said to Warner, and saw the constable's face cloud over instantly. "I couldn't do it behind his back, even if I would like to."

Warner shook his head. "He'll likely not give it."

"He might if I ask him the right way," Runcorn explained. "It'd be hard for him to say no in front of you, and whatever other men he has on the case, and perhaps the vicar as well? Even Mrs. Costain. She was very close to Olivia. It would be hard to explain to her why he refused help."

Warner's eyes widened with sudden understanding, and a new respect. "Well, I'd never have thought of that," he said slowly. "Maybe I'll just have a word with Mrs. Costain, and see as how that can be done. You're a clever man, Mr. Runcorn, and I'm much obliged to have you on our side."

So it was that evening that Runcorn walked up the incline through heavy rain beside Warner and they knocked at the vicarage door a few moments after Sir Alan Faraday had gone inside to inform Mr. and Mrs. Costain of his progress on the case. Warner was due to report also, so the housemaid did not hesitate to take their wet coats and show them both into the parlor where the others were gathered close to the fire.

Naomi Costain looked years older than she had a week ago. Her strong features were deeply marked by grief, her skin so pale she seemed pinched with cold, although the room was warm. She wore black, without ornament of any kind. Her appearance did not seem an ostentatious sign of mourning but simply as if she had not thought about it since the tragic events. Her hair was pinned up and kept out of her way, but it did not flatter her.

Costain himself sat in one of the armchairs, his clerical collar askew, his shoulders hunched. Faraday stood with military stiffness in front of the fire, successfully blocking it from anyone else, but apparently unaware of it. He stared at Warner with a look of hope, then seeing Runcorn behind him, his expression closed over.

"Good evening," he said tersely. "Is there something we can do for you, Mr. Runcorn?" He did not use Runcorn's police rank, although he knew it.

Runcorn assessed the situation. There was no room for prevarication. He must either explain himself, or retreat. He felt foolish for having allowed Warner to do this in front of Costain and his wife. Now his humiliation would be that much more public. Faraday could not afford to lose face in front of others; this had been a tactical error, but it was too late to mend now. He chose his words as carefully as he could, something he was not used to doing.

"It appears to be a far more difficult case than it looked to begin with," he began. "I imagine that this close to Christmas, like everyone else, you are shorthanded, especially of men used to dealing with crime."

The silence was deafening. They were all staring at him, Costain with bewilderment, Naomi with hope, Faraday with contempt.

"This is an island where there is very little crime," Faraday replied. "And even that is mostly the odd theft, or a fight that's more hot temper than cold violence."

"Yes," Costain agreed quickly. "We . . . we've never

had anyone killed . . . so long as I've been here. We've never dealt with anything like this before. What . . . what do you advise?"

Faraday glared at him. His question had been peculiarly tactless.

Runcorn knew to retreat. A word of pride or the slightest suggestion of professional superiority, and he would be excluded in such a way that there would be no room for Faraday to change his mind and ask him back.

"I don't know enough to advise," he said hastily. "All I meant to do was offer whatever help I can, as an extra pair of legs, so to speak."

Faraday moved his weight from one foot to the other, still standing directly in front of the fire.

"Thank you," Naomi said sincerely, breaking the uncomfortable silence.

"To do what?" Faraday asked with an edge to his voice.

Runcorn hesitated, wondering if Faraday's question was a demand that he explain himself, or an oblique and defensive way of asking him for advice. He looked at Faraday, who, as usual, was immaculately dressed, his thick hair neat. But there were hollow shadows smudged around his eyes and a tension in the way he stood which had little to do with the cold. He was in an unenviable position, and with a sudden surge of pity that startled and disconcerted him, Runcorn realized just how out of his depth Faraday was. He had never faced murder before, and people who were frightened and bewildered were looking to him for help he had no idea how to give.

"Ask some of the questions that may lead us towards whoever attacked Miss Costain," he answered. He chose the word "attacked" because it was less brutal than "murdered."

Outside, thunder rolled and the rain beat against the windows.

"Of whom?" Faraday raised his eyebrows. "We have already spoken to all those who live anywhere near the graveyard. Everyone in Beaumaris is appalled by what has happened. They would all help, if they could."

"No, sir," Runcorn spoke before he thought about it. "At least one would not, and maybe many others." He ignored Faraday's scowl, and Costain's wave of denial. "Not because they know who is guilty," he explained. "For other reasons. Everyone has things in their lives they would not share with others: mistakes, embarrassments, events that are private, or which might compromise someone they care for, or to whom they owe a loyalty. It's natural to defend what privacy you have. Everyone does."

Costain sank back in his chair. Perhaps as a minister he was beginning to understand.

Faraday stared. "What are you suggesting, Runcorn? That we dig into everyone's private lives?" He said it with immeasurable distaste.

Again Runcorn hesitated. How on earth could he answer this without either offending Costain and his wife or else retreating until he lost whatever chance he had of conducting a proper investigation? He knew the answer was to be brutal, but he loathed doing it. Only the thought of Olivia lying in the churchyard, soaked in her own blood, and his promise to Melisande, steeled him.

"Until you find the cause of this crime, yes, that is what I am suggesting," he answered, meeting Faraday's blue eyes steadily. "Murder is violent, ugly, and tragic. There is no point investigating it as if it were the theft of a pair of fire dogs or a set of silver spoons. It's the result of hatred or terror, not a moment of misplaced greed."

Costain jerked back as if he had been hit.

"Really!" Faraday protested.

"Mr. Runcorn is quite right," Naomi said softly, her voice sounding with a trace of hesitancy in the quiet room. "We must all put up with a little inconvenience or embarrassment if it is necessary to learn the truth. It is very good of you, Alan, to wish to protect us, and I appreciate your thoughtfulness, but we must face . . . whatever we must to put this behind us."

Faraday waited only a moment, then he turned again to Runcorn. He had no choice but to concede. He got it over with quickly. "Yes. Yes, I regret it, but that does seem to be the situation. Perhaps it would be helpful if you were to give us some of your time, and it is most honorable of you, when I assume you are on holiday. Naturally I shall require you to report to me regularly, not only anything that you may feel you have learned, but also, of course, your intentions for the next step. I had better advise you what we have done so far, and where you should proceed."

"Yes sir," Runcorn said quietly. He had no intention whatsoever of taking instructions from Faraday, who was obviously as concerned with appearances and order as with the darker sides of truth.

Faraday turned to Costain. "If I might speak alone with Runcorn for a few minutes?" he requested. "Is there somewhere suitable?"

"Oh . . . yes, yes, of course." Costain rose wearily to his feet. He looked like an old man, confused, stumbling in both mind and body, although he was barely over fifty. "If you would come this way."

Runcorn excused himself to Naomi, thanking her for her support, nodding to Warner, then he followed Faraday and Costain across the hall to a small study. The fire in this small room was only just dying, still offering considerable warmth, since Faraday didn't resume a position in front of it. Heavy velvet curtains were drawn against the night and the spattering of rain on the glass was almost inaudible here. The walls were lined with bookshelves. Runcorn had a moment to spare in which to notice that, predictably, a large proportion of them were theological, a few on the history or geography of biblical lands, including Egypt and Mesopotamia.

As soon as the door had closed behind Costain again, Faraday turned to Runcorn.

Outside the thunder cracked again.

"I appreciate your help, Runcorn, but let me make this perfectly clear, I will not have you taking over this investigation as if it were some London backstreet. You will not cross-question these good and decent people about their lives as if they were criminals. They are the victims of a hideous tragedy, and deserving of every compassion we can afford them. Do you understand me?" He looked doubtful, as if already he was seeking a way to extricate himself from his decision to allow Runcorn to help.

"Even in London, people are capable of honor and grief when someone they love is murdered," Runcorn said hotly, his good intentions swept away by a protective anger for the people he had known, and for all the other victims of loss, whoever they were. The poor did not love any less or have any different protection from pain.

Faraday flushed. "I apologize," he said gruffly. "That was not what I meant to imply. But these people are my responsibility. You will be as discreet as you can, and report to me every time you make any discovery that could be relevant to Miss Costain's death. Where do you propose to begin?"

"With the family," Runcorn replied. "First I would like to know far more about her than I do. Ugly as it is, she was killed by someone who was standing in front of her, and she was not running from him. She must have known him. Had a stranger accosted her alone at night, in the churchyard, she would have run away, or at the very least have fought. She did neither."

"For God's sake, what are you suggesting?" Faraday said hoarsely. "That someone of her family butchered her? That is unspeakable, and I will not have you . . ."

"I am stating the facts to you," Runcorn cut across him. "Of course I will not put it in those terms to her family. What are you suggesting, sir? That we allow whoever it was to get away with it because looking for him might prove uncomfortable, or embarrassing?"

Faraday was white-faced.

Runcorn had a sudden idea. "If you allow me to ask the ugly questions, Sir Alan, it will at least relieve you of the blame for it. You may then be able to be of some comfort to these families afterwards." He did not quite say that Faraday could blame Runcorn for any offense to their privacy, but the meaning was plain.

Faraday seized it. "Yes, yes I suppose that is so. Then you had better proceed. But for heaven's sake, man, be tactful. Use whatever sensitivity you have."

Runcorn bit back his response. "Yes, sir," he said between his teeth. "I shall begin immediately with Mr. Costain, as soon as you have finished speaking with him yourself."

"For God's sake!" Faraday exploded. "It's already nearly eight o'clock in the evening. Let the poor man have a little peace. Have you no . . ."

"No time to waste," Runcorn concluded for him. "It will be no less upsetting tomorrow."

Faraday gave him a look of intense dislike, but he did not bother to argue any further.

It was no more than quarter of an hour before the door opened and Costain came in alone.

"Please sit down, sir," Runcorn indicated the armchair opposite the desk.

Costain obeyed. The angle of light from the gas lamp on the wall showed the ravages in his face with peculiar clarity.

"I'm sorry to pursue this, Mr. Costain," he began, and he meant it honestly. The vicar's emotions vividly revealed themselves on his aging face. "I will make it as brief as I can."

"Thank you. I would be obliged if you did not have to trouble my wife with this. She and Olivia were . . ."—Costain's voice caught and he needed a moment to regain control—"were very close, more like natural sisters, in spite of the difference in their ages," he finished.

For a moment there was life again in Costain's face as memory flooded back. "They both loved the island. They would walk for miles, especially in the summer. Take a picnic and spend all day away, when duties allowed. My sister was especially fond of wild-flowers. We have many here that one does not find anywhere else. And of course birds. Olivia loved them, too. She would watch them ride the wind."

For an intensely vivid moment Runcorn remembered her face as she had passed him in the aisle of the church, and he found it easy to believe her heart had flown with the birds, her imagination far beyond the reach of earth. No wonder she had been killed with passion. She was the kind of woman who would stir uncontrollable feelings in others: inadequacy, failure, a sense of blindness and frustration, perhaps envy. Not love; love, however unrequited, did not destroy as Olivia had been destroyed.

Costain had overcome his feelings again, at least enough to continue. "But I cannot see how that is of help to you, Mr. Runcorn. Olivia was . . . good-hearted but . . . I regret to say it, undisciplined. She had great compassion, no one was more generous or more diligent in caring for the needy of the parish, whether in goods or in friendship, but she had no true sense of duty."

Runcorn was confused. "Duty?" he questioned.

"Of what is appropriate, of what is . . ." Costain hunted for the word. His face showed how acutely aware he was of their social difference as he searched for a way to explain what he meant without causing offense. "It was already late for her to marry," he said with a slight flush in his cheeks. "She refused many perfectly good offers, without reason except her own . . . willfulness. I had hoped that she would accept Newbridge, but she was reluctant. She wanted something from him quite unrealistic, and I failed to persuade her." The edge of pain in his voice was like a raw wound. "I failed her altogether," he whispered.

"I believe Mr. Barclay also courted her?" Runcorn asked, longing to fill the silence with something more than pity.

"Oh yes. And he would have been an excellent match for her, but she showed no inclination to accept him, either." Costain's shoulders bowed in confusion and defeat.

Runcorn saw Olivia as a beautiful creature refusing to be bound by the walls of convention and other people's perception of her duty. He remembered

Melisande standing in the doorway of her brother's house in London, wanting to help, because she had seen a man leaving the nearby house where a murder had taken place, and Barclay had ordered her inside because he was unwilling that either of them should become involved in something as ugly as murder. He did not care about the bruising to her conscience that she hid. It had probably not even occurred to him. Had he been thinking of her more practical welfare, trying to protect her from dangers she did not see? Or merely protecting himself?

He saw in Costain a man imprisoned in his calling and his social station, bound to duties he had no capacity to meet. Perhaps no one could have. He was too filled with misery to offer Runcorn much more practical help.

"Thank you, sir," Runcorn said as gently as he could. "Would you please ask Mrs. Costain to spare me a few minutes."

Costain looked up sharply. "I asked you not to disturb my wife any further, Mr. Runcorn. I thought you understood that?"

"I wish I could oblige you, sir, but I cannot. She

may be able to tell me of things Miss Costain con-
fided in her, a quarrel, someone who troubled her or
pursued her . . ."

"You are suggesting it was someone my sister
knew! That is preposterous." He stood up.

Runcorn felt brutal. "It was someone she knew,
Mr. Costain. The evidence makes that clear."

"Evidence? Faraday said nothing of that!"

"I will describe it if you wish, but I think it is better if you do not have to hear it."

Costain closed his eyes and seemed to sway on his
feet. Perhaps it was only a wavering of the lamplight. "Please do not tell my wife this." His voice was
no more than a whisper. "Is this why you think Faraday inadequate to the investigation?"

Runcorn was caught off guard. He had had no
idea his opinion was so clear. He certainly had not
meant it to be. Should he lie? Costain deserved better, and he had already seen far more of the truth.

"Yes sir."

"Then do what you have to." Costain turned and
made his way to the door, fumbling with the handle
before he could open it.

Naomi Costain came in a few moments later and closed the door behind her before she sat down. Her face was pale, and in the lamplight the stain of recent tears was visible, even though she had done her best to disguise it. There was a kind of hopelessness in her more eloquent than all the words of loss she might have spoken.

"I will be as brief as I can, ma'am." Runcorn felt a deep sense of intrusion.

"There is no need to," she replied. "Time is of no importance to me. What can I tell you that would help?"

"Mr. Costain said that you and your sister-in-law were very close." He hated his own words, they sounded so trite. "If I knew more about her, I might understand the kind of person who would wish her harm."

She stared into the distance for so long he began to think she was not going to answer, possibly even that she had not understood that it was a question. He drew in his breath to try a different approach when at last she ended the silence.

"She had imagination," she said slowly, testing

each word to be certain it was what she meant. "She would never be told what to think, and my husband found that . . . willful, as if she were deliberately disobedient. I don't believe it was disobedience. I think it was a kind of honesty. But it made her difficult at times."

Runcorn knew little of society, especially on an island like this. He needed to understand the jealousies, the ambitions, the feelings that could escalate into the kind of savagery he had seen perpetrated against her.

"Was there anyone she challenged?" he asked, fumbling for a way to ask what he wanted without hurting her even more. "She was beautiful. Were there men who admired her, women who were rivals?"

Naomi smiled. "You knew her?"

He felt as if some opportunity had passed him by. "No. I saw her once, in church."

The smile faded.

"Oh. Yes, of course. I expect people were envious. It happens, especially against those who do not conform to the way of life expected of them. She did not

have many friends, she grew very impatient sometimes. It is not a good quality. I used to hope she
would learn to curb it, in time." She sighed. "She
liked Mrs. Ewart. At first I thought it was just because she was from London, and brought a touch of
glamour with her. She could speak of the latest plays
and books, music, and that sort of thing. But then I
saw it was deeper than that. They understood something that I did not." A sadness filled her face again,
a kind of loneliness that Runcorn found, to his
amazement, that he understood. It was a knowledge
of exclusion, as if someone had gone and left her
alone in the dark.

"Was she happy?" he asked impulsively.

She looked at him with surprise. "No." Then instantly she regretted it. "I mean that she was rest-
less, she was looking for something. I . . . no, really,
please disregard me, I am talking nonsense. I have
no idea who could have been so deranged by envy or
fear, as to have done such a thing."

He had the overpowering feeling that she was
lying. She knew something she was not prepared to
tell him. "The best thing you can do for her, Mrs.

Costain, is to help us find who killed her," he said urgently.

She rose to her feet, her face weary, her eyes very direct. "Do you believe that it would be best, Mr. Runcorn? How little you know us, or perhaps anyone. You are a good man, but you do not know the wind or the waves of the heart. Landlocked," she added, walking to the door. "You are all landlocked."

It was too late for Runcorn to see anyone else that night, and his mind was in too much confusion to absorb any more. He thanked Costain, and went out into the darkness to walk back to Mrs. Owen's lodging house. The rain had stopped and the wind was bitter, but he was thankful to be alive. He liked the clean smell of the sea, wild as it was, and the absence of human sounds. There were no voices, no clip of horses' hooves, no rattle of wheels, only the hoot of a tawny owl.

*I*t was difficult to gain an interview with Newbridge and it took Runcorn the best part of the morning before he finally stood face-to-face with him in his withdrawing room. The house was old and comfortable. Possibly it had stood in those grounds for two centuries or more, occupied by the one family in times both fat and lean. There were portraits on the walls that bore the same cast of features back to the times of Oliver Cromwell and the Civil War. They were dressed in the ruffles and lace of the Cavaliers. There were no grim-faced, white-collared Puritans.

Some of the furniture had been magnificent in its time, but it now bore marks of heavy use—legs were uneven, one or two surfaces were stained and needed refinishing. But Runcorn had time to notice no more than that before he was aware of Newbridge's impatience.

"What is it you want, Mr. Runcorn?" There was a thickness to his voice and he moved his weight from one foot to the other as though he were anxious to be elsewhere. "I have nothing I can tell you about poor Olivia's death. If I had, I would have told Faraday, for God's sake! Is it not bad enough that we have to live with this tragedy without having to drag out all our memories and our grief over and over again for strangers?" He stood leaning against the mantelshelf, an elegant man, tall and a little lean, with thick wavy hair that grew high from his forehead. His eyes were hazel, deep set, and there was the thin, angry line to his mouth that Runcorn had first noticed in church.

Runcorn found his tolerance already stretched. Loss had different effects on people, and most of them were not attractive. In men it often turned to anger, a kind of suppressed fury as if they had been dealt a blow.

Runcorn bit back his own emotions. "In order to have some better idea of who might have killed her, sir, I need to know more about her. Her family are overweighed with grief just now, and of course they see only one side of her. It is very difficult to speak anything but good of loved ones you mourn. And yet they were also human. She was not killed by accident. Someone was consumed by an unholy rage, and stood face-to-face with her, and even at the last moment, she did not run away. That needs explaining."

Newbridge was very pale and his chest was rising

and falling as if he had climbed to a great altitude and was struggling for breath.

"Are you saying that something in her nature provoked the act, Mr. Runcorn?" he said at last.

"Do you think that impossible?" Runcorn kept his voice low, as though they were confiding in each other.

"Well . . . it's . . . you place me in a terrible situation," Newbridge protested. "How can I observe any decency, and answer such a question?"

"There was no decency in the way she was killed, or indeed, that she was killed at all," Runcorn pointed out.

Newbridge sighed. His face was even paler. "Then you force me in honor to speak more frankly than I would have wished. But if you repeat it to her family, I shall deny it."

Runcorn nodded very slightly.

"She was charming," Newbridge said, looking somewhere away from Runcorn into a distance only he could see. "And beautiful, but I imagine you know that. She was also childish. She was twenty-six, an age when most women are married and have children, and yet she refused to grow up." His body stiffened.

"She would not take any responsibility for herself, which placed an unfair burden upon her brother. I think she took advantage of the fact that he is childless, to remain immature herself, and charge him with her care long past the time when she should have accepted that burden herself."

"Do you think Reverend Costain resented this?"

"He is too good a man to have refused to care for her," Newbridge answered. "And frankly, I think he indulged her. His sense of obligation as a Christian minister was out of proportion. She knew that and took advantage of it."

That was the harshest thing Runcorn had heard said of Olivia, and he was startled how it hurt him. For all he knew, it might be true. Yet he felt as if it was Melisande of whom it had been said. He could think of no reply. He kept his own emotion tightly in check, unaware that he was clenching his muscles and that his nails dug into the palms of his hands.

"Indeed?" he said the word between his teeth.

"Did she make use of anyone else's goodwill in such a way?"

The silence weighed heavily for several moments. Somewhere outside a dog barked, and a gust of rain beat against the windows. The urgency of it brought Newbridge back to the present as if some reverie had been broken. An anger within him came under control, or perhaps it was grief. Runcorn found it impossible to tell, no matter how carefully he watched. He felt intrusive. This man had wanted to marry Olivia. How hard it must be for him to govern his emotions in front of an inquisitive stranger who had seen her hideously dead, but never known or loved her alive.

"She did not, so far as I am aware," Newbridge said finally. "Mrs. Costain was very fond of her, and she had other friends as well. Mrs. Ewart. And Mr. Barclay was courting her. But I imagine you know that. She was friendly with the curate, Kelsall, and various young women in the town, at least in a casual way. Most of them were married, of course, and not free to waste their time in pursuit of dreams, as she did." He looked away from Runcorn again, as if trying to imagine he was not there. "Or to spend hours reading," he went on. "They may have met in charitable work. She was always willing to help those less fortunate, whether they were deserving or not. There was a generosity in her . . ." He stopped abruptly, his head still turned. "Look, I really cannot help you. I have no idea who would want to hurt her, or why. The only possible suggestion I can make is to look more closely at John Barclay. He came to the island only lately. He's a Londoner. Perhaps he lost patience with her indecision. On the other hand, perhaps I merely dislike the man." He faced Runcorn at last. "Now, if you will excuse me, I have nothing further to add. My butler will show you to the door."

*R*uncorn had no choice but to see Barclay next. It was an interview he was not looking forward to, but it was unavoidable. Was it really possible that he had lost his temper with Olivia and faced her in the churchyard with a carving knife? Runcorn disliked the man, but he found that difficult to believe. Runcorn didn't doubt that the man had a hot temper, even that he was capable of delivering a physical blow to another man, but premeditated murder of such bloody violence was beyond even Runcorn's imagination.

Nevertheless, as he walked up the driveway of the great house, sheltered by laurels, his feet crunching on the gravel, he felt a distinct flutter of fear in the pit of his stomach. He did not imagine for an instant that Barclay would attack him, but even if he did, Runcorn had never been a physical coward. He was tall and powerful, and had fought many battles in the streets of the East End in his earlier years. It was the ugliness of misery and hate that frightened him, the brutality of Melisande learning that her brother was capable of such acts, and then having to face the public shame of it. The scandal would follow her as long as she lived, not from any guilt of hers, but by association.

But if Runcorn were to evade it now, even for her sake, then he betrayed himself, and the principles he believed in and had sworn an oath to uphold. He was a servant of the law and the people, and as he stood on the front step of this beautiful house on the Isle of

Anglesey, as if it were a crossroads in the journey of his mind, this was more important than pleasing anyone else. If he foreswore that, then after he had parted from Melisande and left Anglesey, he would have nothing left.

The butler answered the door and invited Runcorn to go into the morning room, saying he would inform Mr. Barclay of his presence.

Runcorn accepted and followed the man's stiff figure across the parquet floor to the faded, comfortable room facing onto a side garden. A fire was lit and several armchairs were pulled into a ring around it. Two bookcases were filled with volumes that looked as if they had seen much use. A bowl of holly leaves and berries sat on a low table. Runcorn knew it was a house taken only for the season, but it had an air of being lived in with ease and a certain familiarity.

Barclay appeared after nearly quarter of an hour, but he seemed in an agreeable mood and made no objection to Runcorn having called without prior appointment.

"Learn anything yet?" he asked conversationally, coming in and closing the door.

Runcorn found himself relaxing a little. He realized Melisande must have prepared the way for him, at least as much as she could. He should respond with tact, for her sake.

"It appears that Miss Costain was a more complex person than we had at first assumed," he replied.

Barclay shrugged. "One always wishes to speak well of the dead, particularly when they have died violently, and young. It's a natural kind of decency, almost like laying flowers." He did not sit, or invite Runcorn to, so they both remained standing at opposite sides of the fire.

It was Runcorn's turn to speak. He tried to frame his questions as if he were asking for assistance. "I am trying to find out as much as I can about where everyone was, leading up to the time she was killed. Something must have caused it to happen . . ."

Barclay's face registered a quick understanding. "You mean a quarrel, or a discovery, that kind of thing?"

"Exactly." Runcorn was glad to be able to agree. "Constable Warner has already done a great deal in that line, but I was wondering if you could help any further. You knew Miss Costain. Were you aware of any events that day, anyone she saw, or anyone who was angry or distressed with her?" He was not sure what he expected. For the time being, simply to talk was good. He could move slowly from small facts to larger passions.

Barclay gave it some thought. "She could be a difficult woman," he said after a while. "A dreamer rather than a realist, if you know what I mean?" He met Runcorn's eyes. "Some women are a trifle impractical, especially if they have always been cared for by a father or elder brother, and never had to consider the real world. Olivia . . . Olivia was spoiled. She was charming and generous. She could be an excellent companion. But there was in her a streak of willfulness, a clinging onto childhood dreams and fancies which could become tedious after a while. I felt for Costain." He gave a slight shrug, as if confiding an understanding better implied than spoken.

"Did they quarrel?" Runcorn asked.

"Oh for heaven's sake, not to the point where he would take a knife and follow her up to the graveyard and kill her!" Barclay looked appalled. "But I'm sure she tested his patience sorely. It is not an easy thing to be responsible for one's sister. You have a father's distress and obligation without a father's authority." He spread his hands in a gesture of futility. "I don't doubt for an instant that he did the best he could, but she was flighty, unrealistic, apparently unaware of her own responsibilities in return."

He gave a slight smile. "Made me grateful that my own sister is so much more sensible. Faraday will make an excellent husband for her. He has every quality one could desire. He is of fine family, he can provide for her both financially and socially. He is of spotless reputation, good temperament, altogether a thoroughly decent fellow. And fine looking as well, which is hardly necessary, but it is very agreeable. Melisande is a beautiful woman, and could take her pick from quite a few. I'm most grateful that she has more good sense than Olivia had, and does not entertain absurd fancies." He held Runcorn's gaze and smiled steadily and coldly.

Runcorn's head was crowded with an avalanche of thoughts and feelings, bruising him, crushing sense and rational meaning. He struggled to think of something to say that was sensible, purely practical, and would remove that smirk from Barclay's lips.

"You are right," the words were thick and clumsy on his tongue. "A sane man does not murder his sister because she is disinclined to marry the suitor he has chosen for her. But have you ever had a suggestion that Costain may not be entirely sane?"

Barclay's smile vanished. "No, of course not. Olivia could at times try the patience of even a good man, but her brother is beyond reproach. If he were a man less devoted to decency, less governed by the affections of a brother and more of a lover, or would-be lover, then he might be less . . . sane." He lifted his shoulders very slightly. "Thank God it is not my trade or my duty to find out who killed her. I cannot think of anything more unsavory than hunting through the sins and griefs of other people's lives in search of the final depravity, but I appreciate that someone has to do it if we are to have the rule of law. If I can be of assistance to you, then naturally I shall do what I can."

"Thank you," Runcorn said bleakly.

Barclay dismissed his thanks with a gesture of his hand, and before Runcorn could frame the next question, he continued. "I would be obliged if you did not harass my sister with this any more than is absolutely necessary. She was fond of Miss Costain. They had certain situations in life in common, and Melisande is a soft-hearted woman, at times a trifle naïve. She was inclined to believe whatever Olivia told her, and I fear it was not always the truth. Olivia was not a good influence." His smile returned.

"I am glad that Melisande is committed to Faraday, and will soon be settled. Perhaps she would have been able to prevail upon Olivia, had she lived. But that is tragically of no importance any more. If I can think further, I shall certainly inform you." He turned the corners of his mouth down. "Unpleasant word, inform. Sounds as if it were clandestine, somehow deceitful, but then, to defend someone guilty of such a crime would be even worse, wouldn't it?" It was half a question, the answer assumed.

Runcorn found the words sticking in his throat, but he had to force himself to agree. "Yes sir, I regret that murder frequently exposes many smaller sins that can change the quality of our lives forever afterwards."

Barclay stared at him, an expression in his eyes that was impossible to read: anger, triumph, a knowledge of his own power, an uncertainty.

"Thank you, Mr. Barclay," Runcorn said quietly. "I appreciate your assistance. I wish everyone were as honorable in their duty."

If Barclay detected any sarcasm, he did not show it even by a flicker.

The curate, Thomas Kelsall, was utterly different. His slender figure was bent forward as he walked and there was tension in the angle of his shoulders. Runcorn caught up with him as he strode doggedly through the pounding rain on his visits to the parish's old and needy. Some of them would normally be Costain's duty, but considering the circumstances, young Kelsall had taken it upon himself.

"You may think it arrogant of me," he said to Runcorn as they kept pace with each other. "Some people might prefer to see the minister himself, but just now not only is he spending time with poor Mrs. Costain, but he does not know how to answer people. What can they say to him? That they are sorry? That she was the most charming, the most vividly alive person they ever knew, and her death is like God taking some of the light from the world?" He kept his face resolutely forward. "And what can he say, except agree, and try to keep from embarrassing them with his pain? It is better I go. At least they do not feel as if they have to comfort me. I can address their problems, which is what I am there for."

"But you did know her well, and feel her death very hard." Runcorn knew it was brutal, but stretching it out with euphemisms would be like pulling a bandage off slowly. And it was less honest.

"We were friends," Kelsall replied simply. "We could speak to each other about all manner of things, without having to pretend we felt differently. If something was funny we laughed, even if sometimes people like the vicar thought it was inappropriate. He was her brother, and my superior, but our eyes would meet and we would each know the other thought the same. We both understood what it was to have dreams . . . and regrets." His voice trembled a little. "I cannot imagine I will ever like anyone else quite so much, so fully."

Runcorn looked sideways at him, plunging forward into the wind and rain, and did not know for certain whether it was tears that wet his cheeks or the weather. They reached the house of one elderly parishioner, and Runcorn waited outside shivering in the lee of the porch until Kelsall returned. They set out walking again.

"Is it true that she refused Mr. Newbridge's offer of marriage?" Runcorn asked after forty or fifty paces.

Kelsall hunched his shoulders and walked more intently forward. Thunder rumbled around the horizon. "She was a woman of deep feelings," he said, shaking his head a little and fumbling for the right words. "Visionary. You could never have tied her down to petty things. It would have broken her. He couldn't see that. He didn't love her, he liked what he thought she was, and did not look closely enough to see that he was utterly wrong. I don't think he even . . . listened." He looked suddenly at Runcorn. "Why do people marry someone they don't even listen to? How can they bear to be so lonely?" He was shuddering, waving his hands as he strode. "Of course she refused him. What else could she do?"

Runcorn did not reply. In his mind for a moment he saw the face of the girl in green as she had passed him in church, then he saw Melisande, and the bland, handsome features of Faraday, and he was filled with the same helpless despair that he heard in Kelsall. Had the curate loved Olivia? Would it have been infinitely more than friendship if he could have chosen? Was there a completely different kind of hunger beneath the grief he displayed in his young, vulnerable face?

They walked together without speaking again, and he left Kelsall at his next parishioner's house.

Making his way back up the incline again to find Warner, he did not change his mind. He still thought Kelsall a friend, but perhaps a closer one, more observant, more of a confidante than he had at first assumed.

The redwings were gone from the field. He hoped they would be back after the rain.

He spent the afternoon with Warner, but the only thing that emerged from their efforts was that Kelsall's alibi was finally confirmed by the absent-minded old gentleman he had been visiting, who had been up late with the croup.

In the late afternoon, just before dusk, there was a sudden lifting of the clouds and the air was filled with the soft, warm light of the low sun, already touching the high ground with a patina of gold. Suddenly the sea was blue and the Menai Strait a shining mirror barely wind-rippled as the icy breath of the sky whispered across it and disappeared.

Runcorn started to walk again, drawn towards the shore. It was cold, but he did not mind. There was a simplicity to it, a perfect melting of solid earth with the living, changing sea, a boundlessness of one into the other.

He turned and craned his neck upwards as he watched gulls soaring inland on the invisible currents, careening sideways and slipping down and then up, looking effortless as they mounted into the light and were lost to view.

It was almost silent, a faint whisper of water behind him. London had never offered him such infinite peace. There was always noise, some kind of clatter of human occupation, an end to vision, to possibility.

He began climbing upwards, away from the shore. Perhaps he was wrong, and he had allowed himself to believe in limits where there were none, except those he made for himself. He thought of the past with a different view, almost as if he were regarding someone else. He saw in himself a man of practical common sense, one whose judgment of character was usually right but without empathy. He lacked a passion, an understanding of dreams. Had he guarded himself from such things, afraid to face his own smallness? He had hated Monk's anger and his fire, his impatience with stupidity, his arrogance. Or more truly, was he afraid of it, because it challenged the conformity that was so much less dangerous?

Was that what Olivia had done, too, challenged

conformity? She had climbed these hills, he knew that from Naomi Costain. She might even have stood on this level stretch of the path and stared at the fire of the setting sun, as he was doing, and looked at the horizon where the sky and the sea became one.

Thinking of Olivia, Runcorn realized that small people like himself who want to be safe, who have no driving hunger, are afraid of those who upset their world, remove the boundaries that close them in and excuse their cowardice. He had hated Monk for that. Who had hated Olivia? Not Naomi. But what about Costain? Did she question this edifice of his faith, the daily justification of his status, his income, his reason for being? Could he forgive her for that?

Or was he simply a good man who did not understand a difficult sister who was his responsibility to feed and clothe, and keep within society's bounds, for her own sake?

The sun was a scarlet ball on the horizon, and even as he watched, it dropped below the rim, spilling fire across the sea. He decided he would stand here as darkness gathered and closed in, wondering what Olivia had felt. What visions had she seen, and perhaps died for? Was Melisande anything like her, except in his imagination? But he was a practical man, trained from years of making himself fit the mold of necessity, and the only real service he could perform now was to discover the truth. It might help no one to name the guilty, but it was surely a necessary service to free the innocent from blame, of others and their own.

*I*n the morning Runcorn rose early and ate the rich breakfast Mrs. Owen cooked for him. She seemed to enjoy filling the plate to overflowing with bacon, eggs, and potato cakes, then watching him make his way through it. He did not really want so much, and initially he ate it only to satisfy her sense of hospitality. But in succeeding days, as he worked his way through the meal he had talked to her and learned with growing interest her opinions of various people in the village and involved in the case. Her perception was simple, but sometimes surprisingly acute.

"Just the right man for the vicarage here, Mr. Costain is," she said. "Poor soul, his wife. Lonely I think. No children. Doesn't know how to talk without really saying anything, if you know what I mean? People don't always want to think. Like Miss Olivia, she was."

Runcorn had his mouth full and was unable to ask her to explain further, and he worried that if he did, she might think that perhaps she had said too much, and be more discreet in the future.

"Like some more tea, Mr. Runcorn?" she offered, the pot in her hand.

"Helps a lot of things, from a headache to a broken heart. Lovely girl, Miss Olivia was. Quick to sorrow, and quick to joy, God rest her. Never found anyone for herself, that I know of, in spite of what they said."

Runcorn swallowed his mouthful whole and nearly choked himself. "What did they say?" he asked huskily, reaching for the tea to wash it down.

"Just silly gossip," she replied. "Nothing to it. Would you like another piece of toast, Mr. Runcorn?"

He declined, finished his tea, and set out to look for Kelsall. This time he found the curate in the church, tidying up.

"Do you know something new?" he asked, striding towards Runcorn, black cassock swinging.

Runcorn felt a twinge of failure, as if he should have done better. "Not yet."

"Perhaps if we leave, we will not be interrupted," Kelsall suggested. "Here I am always 'on duty,' as it were. It's cold outside, but at least it's not raining." He suited his actions to the words without waiting to see if Runcorn agreed. In the graveyard he matched his steps to Runcorn's and guided their way out of the gate and onto a road leading out of the village towards the open hillside.

"Why do people kill others, Mr. Runcorn?" he asked. "I have been thinking of it all night. If any man knows, it is surely you. It is such a . . . a barbarous and futile way to solve anything."

Runcorn looked at his earnest face and knew that the question was perfectly serious. Perhaps it was one he should have asked himself in more detail days ago. "Several reasons," he said thoughtfully. "Sometimes it is greed, for money, for power, for property such as a house. Sometimes for something as trivial as an ornament or a piece of jewelry."

"Not Olivia," Kelsall said with certainty. "She had no possessions of any note. She was entirely dependent on her brother."

"Ambition," Runcorn continued. "It can drive people to violence, or betrayal."

"Olivia's death helps no one," Kelsall responded. "Anyway, there is nothing around here to aspire to. It is all predictable, small offices, of no great power."

Runcorn turned over all the past cases he could think of, particularly those of passion. "Jealousy," he said grimly. "She was beautiful, and from what people say, she had a quality unlike anyone else, a fire and a courage different from others of her age and position. That can also make people feel uncomfortable, even threatened. People can kill out of fear."

Kelsall walked on in silence. "What kind of fear?" he said at last.

Runcorn heard the change in his voice and knew that suddenly they were treading delicately, on the edge of truth. He must act slowly, he might be about to rip the veil from a pain that the young man had been keeping well covered.

"All kinds," he said, watching Kelsall's face in profile, his eyes and the lines of his mouth half hidden. "Sometimes it is of physical pain, but more often it is fear of loss."

"Loss," Kelsall tasted the word carefully. "What sort of loss?"

Runcorn did not answer, hoping Kelsall would suggest something himself.

They walked another fifty paces. The wind was easing off, although the clouds were low and dark to the east.

"You mean fear of scandal?" Kelsall asked. "Or ridicule?"

"Certainly. Many victims of blackmail have killed their tormentors." Was this what had happened? Perhaps Olivia had learned a secret that somebody was afraid she would use against them. He looked at

Kelsall as closely as he dared, but he could see no change in the curate's expression. He still looked hurt and confused.

There was no sound but the wind in the grass and, far away, the echo of waves breaking on the rocks.

"Olivia wasn't like that," Kelsall said finally. "She would never repeat anyone's secrets, still less would she use them. What for? The things she wanted could not be bought."

"What did she want?"

"Freedom," he said without hesitating to think. "She wanted to be herself, not the person convention said she should be. Perhaps we all want it, or think we do, but few of us are prepared to pay the price. It hurts to be different." He stopped and faced Runcorn. "Is that why she was murdered, because she made other people aware of how ordinary they were, how easily they denied their dreams?"

"I doubt it," Runcorn said gently. "Wouldn't someone able to see that quality in her also know that killing her would make no difference whatever to their own . . . futility?"

"Not if she laughed at them," Kelsall replied.

"Some people cannot bear to be mocked. Ridicule can hurt beyond some people's power to bear, Mr. Runcorn. It strikes the very core of who you believe yourself to be. One can forgive many things, but not being made to see yourself as ridiculous, a coward at life. That kind of rage is acid in the soul."

Was he speaking of himself? Runcorn almost wondered for a moment if he was on the brink of hearing a confession. It would hurt. He genuinely liked the young man. He had seen his gentleness with the frail and old, help given as a privilege, not a duty.

"What do you know, Mr. Kelsall?" he asked. "I think it is time you spoke the truth."

"I know that Newbridge and Barclay were at daggers drawn over her, but I don't know if either of them really even wanted her, or simply hated each other because the battle was public. Some people do not take to losing with grace."

Runcorn struggled to follow. "If that were so, would they not kill each other, rather than her?"

Kelsall shrugged, and started walking again. "I suppose so. Or even Faraday. Although it's a bit late for that now."

"The chief constable?" Runcorn caught up with him. "What has he to do with it?"

"Oh, he courted her too, a while ago," Kelsall replied. "The poor vicar thought that would have been an excellent match, even though he was quite a few years older than she. He thought it would settle her down a bit. But she gave him no encouragement at all, and he soon grew tired of it."

"Faraday?" the word burst from Runcorn in amazement, and a kind of dull and momentary anger. He had courted Olivia, and now he was going to marry Melisande. Olivia had refused him. And Melisande had been obliged to accept him.

Runcorn was being ridiculous, he knew it, and still his thoughts raced on. He might have lost interest in Olivia because she was flighty, a dreamer, irresponsible. He might love Melisande because she was gentler, a visionary still capable of loving the real, the human and fallible. A woman not only beautiful but brave enough to accept an ordinary man, and perhaps in time make of him something greater.

Kelsall was still talking, but Runcorn had stopped

paying attention. He had to ask the curate to repeat himself, and to drag his own attention back to the one thing he was good at, the skill that gave him his identity.

"You said something about Mr. Barclay," he prompted.

Kelsall shook his head a little. "I think the vicar envies him."

"Why?" Although he feared that he knew the answer.

Kelsall smiled without pleasure. "Barclay's sister does not argue with him. He has a way of making her understand what has to be done, what life requires of us, if we are to survive. I think Barclay would have persuaded Olivia as well, only he stopped wishing to, just before she died. I have no idea why, or I would have told you. The vicar thought Barclay a fine match for her. Only Mrs. Costain did not care for him." He gave a slight shrug. "But then, she did not care for Newbridge, either, so far as I could see. The vicar accused her of wishing Olivia to remain single because she was such a good companion. But of course it was no good for her. She should marry and have her own home, and children, like any other woman. And to be honest, it is something of an expense on a clergyman's stipend to dress and provide for two women." He looked deeply unhappy. "Fear of poverty is not the same thing as greed, Mr. Runcorn. Really, it is not."

"No," Runcorn said quietly. "No, it is a very human and natural thing. Perhaps Miss Costain was not aware of the drain she was on his resources."

"No. I think she was not always very practical," Kelsall conceded. "It takes a long time for a man of the cloth to earn enough to keep a wife, never mind a sister as well." There was loneliness and self-mockery in his voice, and he did not meet Runcorn's eyes.

"Or a policeman," Runcorn responded. "But then a policeman's wife would expect far less." There was self-mockery in his words too. On his salary he could not keep a woman like Melisande for a month, let alone a lifetime. It was not only social class that divided them, or experience and beliefs—it was money and all it could buy, the comforts a woman of Melisande's background accepted without even noticing them.

Kelsall caught the shadow of Runcorn's pain, and looked at him with new intensity and a sudden flame of gentleness in his eyes. He was tactful enough to say nothing.

*R*uncorn reported to Faraday just before dark as he had been commanded to do. It was an uncomfortable interview, and largely fruitless. He was leaving the vicarage and walking across the churchyard when Melisande caught up with him. She had come out of the house hastily and had no cloak with her. The wind blew her hair off her face and whipped long strands of it out of its pins. It looked soft, giving her a dark, wild halo and showing the pallor of her skin. She was frightened, he could see it in her eyes, but he did not know if it was for herself, or for the ugly things she could see unraveling before her, pulled at by the fingers of violent death.

He longed to be able to comfort her, and found himself wordless, standing there among the grass in the wind.

"Mr. Runcorn," she said urgently. "Forgive me for following you, but I wished so much to speak with you without my brother knowing. Might we go into the lee of the church?"

"Of course." He wondered whether to offer her his arm over the uneven ground. He would like to feel her touch, even through the thickness of his jacket. He could imagine it. But what if she refused? She might think it was impertinent. It was asking for humiliation to assume more than plain politeness, even for an instant. He kept his arm by his side and walked stiffly over to the shelter of the church walls. The silence was so painful that he started to speak as soon as they were there.

"I am learning a great deal more about Miss Costain." He told her most of what Kelsall had said, but more gently phrased, and he did not mention that Faraday had courted her, too, although he wondered if perhaps she knew. "It seems she was unwilling to accept any marriage her brother recommended for her," he finished. "And it was causing some ill-feeling, and a degree of financial stress."

"You mean Mr. Newbridge?" she said quickly.

He did not know how to answer. He had been clumsy. In trying to tell her something of meaning he had put himself in a position where either he had to lie or admit that it also meant her brother, and her own suitor.

Too quickly she understood. Her smile was self-mocking. "And John," she added. "It is no secret that he courted her as well, although I think he became a little disillusioned with her some short time before her death. I think he requires in a woman more sense of the practical than she was willing to give." She looked away from him and sighed in exasperation. "I'm sorry, that is such a foolish euphemism. Olivia was an individual, she had the courage at least to attempt to live her dreams. They were not so very unreasonable. She wanted to travel, but she would have worked to achieve that. Of course a vicar's sister is not supposed to work at anything. What is there that a respectable woman can do?" There was an ache of longing in her voice, as if she were speaking of herself, not a friend she understood too well.

"She had no real skills, and not a great deal of practical knowledge of the world," she continued.

"One cannot survive without at least some money. If one had been born poor one might at least have learned to do something useful. Sometimes I wonder if necessity might not be a better spur than dreams, don't you think?" Without warning she turned to look at him, meeting his eyes with fierce candor. "Do you like what you do, Mr. Runcorn?"

He was at a loss to answer her. He could feel his face flaming, as if she would see his emotions drowning him. "I . . . not always. I . . . it . . ." This was his one chance to be honest with her. "Sometimes it is terrible, painful, you see awful things, and cannot help."

"Isn't that better than seeing nothing at all?" she demanded. "And at least you can try!"

She was so vivid he almost felt as if he were touching her in the sharp air. Suddenly the words came easily.

"Yes. And at times I succeed. I can't bring back the dead, and catching the guilty doesn't always make sense, or justice, but it eases, and it explains. Understanding gets rid of the sense of confusion, the helplessness to know what happened and why."

She smiled. "You are fortunate. You have something worth doing, even if you don't always manage to complete it, at least you know you have tried."

He had never thought of it like that. Barclay had defined his job as clearing up the detritus of other people's crimes and follies, a sort of sweeper-up of dirt. Melisande clearly saw something more. "Is that how you see it?" he asked uncertainly.

She shook her head. "Oh, don't think of John. Sometimes he takes pleasure in being offensive. He denigrates what he doesn't understand. It's a kind of . . . fear. We are all afraid of something, if we are honest."

"What was Olivia afraid of?" He hardly dared ask. Were they even speaking of Olivia, or of Melisande herself?

She looked away again. "Of loneliness," she answered. "Of failure. Of coming to the end of your life and realizing all the passionate, beautiful things you could at least have tried to do, but you didn't have the courage. And then it's too late . . ." She stopped, not as if she had no further thought, but as if she could not bear to speak it aloud.

Perhaps he should have turned to the stark outline of the church, or even to the carved and orna-
mental gravestones beyond, but he did not. Her grief
filled the air, and he knew it was not only a compassion for Olivia but also an acute awareness of her
own suffering and emptiness. He had never so intensely wanted to touch anyone, but he knew he
could not, not even the cold, ungloved hand at her
side. There was no comfort he could offer except his
skill, and now he was increasingly afraid that what
he might learn further of Barclay would prove uglier
than she could imagine.

But he, too, had to follow the truth, wherever it
led. This wide, clean land with its endless distances
had awoken a disturbing awareness of his own defi-
ciencies, the narrowness that Monk had so despised.
Suddenly he wanted to change, for himself, not even
for dreams of Melisande, however sweet or hopeless.
He was aware of a gaping hole, of a loss he could feel
but not name. The silence of the air was a balm, but
something inside him ached to be filled.

"I'll find him," he said aloud to her. "But it will not
be comfortable. It will show hatred you did not know

was there, and weakness you had not had to look at before. I'm sorry."

"I know," she accepted. "It is foolish, like a small child, to imagine it is something out there, a piece of madness that just happened to strike us. It comes from inside. Thank you for being so honest." She hesitated a moment as if to add something else, then simply said good night, and with a brief smile, was gone.

He took a step after her, not knowing if he should walk beside her at least back to the gate of the big house. Then he realized the foolishness of such an act. She had sought him in the tumble of gravestones, and then the lee of the church, precisely not to be seen.

He turned and made his way back to Mrs. Owen, and something hot to eat and drink.

*I*n the morning he reported again to Faraday, who received him with a look of hope that he had at last found some concrete evidence. His expression died as soon as he saw Runcorn's face.

"I think you misunderstood me, Runcorn," he said tartly. "There really is no need to keep coming here to tell me that you have learned nothing."

Runcorn felt the chill and, for an instant, the thoughtless, ill-expressed temper he would have exhibited a year ago was hot inside him. He choked it down.

"I had a long talk with Kelsall, sir, and he clarified a great many things in my mind."

Faraday gave him a sour look of disbelief, but he did not interrupt. His expression said vividly what he considered Runcorn's mind to be worth, if a conversation with the curate could improve it.

Runcorn felt himself coloring. He knew his voice was tart, but it was beyond his control. "He asked the nature of motives for murder. They are generally simple: greed, fear, ambition, revenge, outrage . . ."

"Get to your point, Runcorn. What does that tell us that we did not already know? She was hardly threatening to anyone."

"Not physically, sir, but in reputation or belief, in challenge to authority, in threat to expose what is private, shameful, or embarrassing," Runcorn explained.

"Oh. You think perhaps Miss Costain was privy to someone's secrets? She would not have betrayed such a thing. If you had known her, you would not even suggest it."

"Not even if it were illegal?"

Faraday frowned. "Who? Whose secrets would she know? I shall have to ask Costain."

"No, sir!"

"Surely he is the most likely to know who . . . Good God!" Faraday's eyes inclined. "You don't think he—"

"I don't know," Runcorn cut him off. "But that is not the only kind of fear. There is the dread of humiliation, of being mocked, of having one's inadequacies laid bare."

"That seems a bit fanciful," Faraday said, but the color in his cheeks belied his words.

"Newbridge courted her, and she rejected him," Runcorn observed, making it a statement. "So, apparently, did John Barclay."

Faraday chewed his lips. "Do you think he is capable of such violence?"

"Did she reject him also?" Runcorn continued.

"Yes, I believe so. Surely he couldn't . . ." His eyes widened, the question already answered in his mind.

Runcorn saw it and anger burned up inside him for Melisande. This man was going to marry her, and yet in order to solve a murder he was willing to believe that her brother could be guilty. Or did it reflect a closer knowledge of Barclay than Runcorn had, especially during the time of his acquaintance with Olivia? Was he finally facing a grief he had tried to avoid, but could not any longer?

"You know him better than I do," Runcorn said with a greater gentleness. "How did he accept her rejection? Did he love her deeply?"

Faraday looked startled.

It raced through Runcorn's mind that what he dreamed of as love was not something Faraday even considered. There was no understanding of the passion, the hunger, the tenderness, the soaring of the heart or the plunge of despair. He was thinking of an arrangement, an affection. Runcorn was harrowed up with a rage so intense he could have struck Faraday's smug, bland face and beaten his assumptions out of him. He wanted to feel blood and bone under his fists.

Were these the feelings Olivia's murderer had felt? Only they had used a carving knife? Why? Was the killer a woman? Someone with no physical power to strike, but the passion nevertheless?

"It doesn't have to be a man," he said aloud. "Who else did Newbridge court? Or John Barclay? Who could have loved or wanted them with such fierce possessiveness?"

"A woman?" Faraday was stunned. "But it was . . . violent! Brutal."

"Women can be just as brutal as men," Runcorn said tartly. "It happens less often, simply for opportunity and perhaps schooling, but the rage is just as savage, and when it breaks through the years of self-control, it will be uglier."

"Jealousy?" Faraday tasted the idea. Now he was meeting Runcorn's eyes and there was no evasion in him, no weariness. "Over Newbridge? I don't think so. Although to be honest, I hadn't considered it. I'll have Warner look into it more closely. John Barclay, that seems possible. He can be very charming, and he has a high opinion of himself. He would not take rejection easily."

"I heard from Kelsall that it was he who rejected Miss Costain," Runcorn corrected him.

Faraday shrugged with a slight smile. "That may be what she told him," he replied. "They were friends. She might not wish him to think she had been rebuffed. She was a difficult young woman, Runcorn. If you intend to solve her murder, you must recognize that. She was a dreamer, impractical, selfish, very willful in certain matters. She steadily refused to be guided by her brother, a patient and long-suffering man where she was concerned, and I regret to say, not always best supported by his wife. John Barclay is much more fortunate, and I daresay wiser, even if he has a certain vanity."

With the very reference to Melisande, Runcorn felt the iron vise close around her as if it were around himself. In his mind he stood with her again in the churchyard and heard her voice speaking of Olivia, the emotion trembling in it, and he knew this fear was also for herself. But Melisande was a woman who obeyed necessity, understanding there was no choice. Olivia had rebelled. Were they connected? How? It still formed no pattern he could read to be certain of innocence or guilt.

"Thank you," Faraday said briskly, cutting across his thoughts. "The fact that it might have been a woman would explain why Miss Costain was not at first afraid of her. Also, of course, all those we have questioned would have been thinking in terms of men." His shoulders eased and he smiled momentarily. "Thank you, Runcorn. I am obliged for your expert opinion, and of course for your time."

*R*uncorn was unsatisfied. He had raised questions to Faraday; he had not given answers. How much was he seeing of the woman Olivia Costain had been, and how much was his picture of her colored by Kelsall's feelings for her? How much was his feeling for Melisande? He was not doing his job. He had in the far distant past criticized Monk for emotions, usually impatience and anger, and now he was guilty of them himself. How Monk would mock him!

And then with surprise, a lurch into freedom—he realized that he did not care. He could be hurt by other people's opinions of him, but he could no longer be twisted or destroyed by them.

Moreover, he realized that he could learn more of Olivia Costain's life from those less close to her, those who could see her with clearer eyes. And in doing that, he would also discreetly learn a great deal more about Alan Faraday as well. If there really was a violent and terrible envy, it could as easily be over him. And that might even mean that Melisande was in danger, too.

Should he warn her? Of what? He had no idea.

Just then, as he walked down the steep, winding road towards the town, he realized that in fact he did not believe it was a woman jealous of Olivia, so much as a woman afraid of her. She challenged the order of things. She was a disruption in the midst of certainty, the old ways mocked and the rules broken.

But who cared about that enough to kill the trespasser, the blasphemer? That could be a woman. Or a man whose power and authority was vested in the rules that do not change. Whoever he was he could even feel himself justified in getting rid of her, before she destroyed even more.

The vicar, Costain? The chief constable, Faraday? Or Newbridge, the lord of the manor, with roots centuries deep in the land.

He paused before a house where he had never stopped before, then finally knocked. The woman who answered was white-haired and bent nearly double over her cane, but her eyes were unclouded and she had no difficulty hearing him when he spoke. "Miss Mendlicott?"

"Yes I am. And who are you, young man? You sound like a Londoner to me. If you're lost, no use asking me the way, all the roads are new since I went anywhere."

"I'm not lost, Miss Mendlicott," he replied. "It is you I would like to speak to. And you are right, I am from London. I'm in the police there, but it is about the death of Miss Costain I want to ask you. You taught her in school, didn't you?"

"Of course I did. I taught them all. But if I knew

who had killed her, you wouldn't have had to come looking for me, young man, I've had sent for you. Don't keep me standing here in the cold. What's your name? I can't go on calling you 'young man.'" She squinted up at him. "Not that you're so young, are you!"

"Superintendent Runcorn, Miss Mendlicott. And thank you, I would like to come in." He did not tell her he was fifty. That made him twenty years older than Melisande.

She led him into a small sitting room with barely space for two chairs, but pleasantly warm. On the mantelshelf there was a small jug with fresh primroses and a spray of rosemary. Anglesey was always surprising him.

He told her without evasion that he wished to learn more of the men who had courted Olivia, and whom she had refused.

"Poor child," the old lady said sadly. "Understood everything, and nothing. Could name most of the birds in the sky when she was fourteen, and had no idea how few other people even looked at them. Blind as a bat, she was."

Runcorn struggled to keep up with her. "You mean she was naïve?"

"I mean she couldn't see where she was going!" Miss Mendlicott snapped. "Of course she was naïve. Nothing wrong with her eyesight. Didn't want to look."

"Did Sir Alan Faraday court her seriously, do you know?"

"Handsome boy," she said, staring beyond him into the winter garden with its bare trees. "Good at cricket, as I recall. Or so someone told me. Never watched it myself. Couldn't make head nor tail of it."

"Did he court Miss Costain?" he repeated the question.

"Of course he did. But she had no patience with him. Nice man, but tedious. She used to tell me about him. Came to see me every week. Brought me jam." Her eyes filled with tears, and unashamed, she let them slide down her cheeks.

"She talked about Sir Alan to you?"

"Done well for himself," she said, shaking her head a little. "Grew up here, then went south to the mainland."

"England?"

She gave him a withering look. "Wales, boy! Wales!"

He smiled in spite of himself. "But Olivia refused him."

"Course she did. Liked him well enough. Kind man, when you get to know him, she said. Good horseman, patient, light hands. Need that on a horse. Heavy hands ruin a horse's mouth. Loves the land. Best thing about him," she said.

"But she refused his offer of marriage?" He did not want to see Faraday as part of this wide, beautiful land with its wind and its endless distance, when Runcorn himself had to leave it and go back to the clatter and smoke of London. But he did want to think that there was a better side to him, a man who could love and give of himself, who could be gentle, handle power with a light touch.

"Was he angry that she refused him?" he persisted.

She looked at him as if he were a willfully obtuse student. "Of course he was. Wouldn't you be? You offer a beautiful and penniless young woman your name and your place in society, your wealth and your loyalty, and she says she does not wish for it!"

He tried to imagine the scene. Had he loved her? He certainly had not shown it when he spoke of her after her death. Had he forgotten her in his new love for Melisande? That was too raw in his mind to touch. "Why did she refuse him? Was there someone else she preferred?"

Miss Mendlicott smiled. "Not in any practical way. Sometimes she had very little sense. She could see the flowers in front of her, count their petals, and she could see the stars, and tell you their names. But she was fuzzy about the middle distance, as if there were mist over the field." There were tears in her eyes again and she did not brush them away. She was not going to dissemble or excuse herself to a man from London, probably not to anyone else, either.

"There was someone impractical," he concluded aloud. Had that been Kelsall after all, a young man who could still barely afford to keep himself, let alone a wife?

"A poet," she replied. "And explorer." She snorted.

"Of all the romantic and ridiculous things to be. Off to the Mountains of the Moon, he was."

"What?" He was jolted out of courtesy by shock.

"Africa!" the old lady said witheringly. "Some of these explorers have very fanciful minds. Heaven knows where they would have ended up, if she had gone with him."

"She wanted to?" It was surprisingly painful to ask, because he could imagine the loneliness of being left behind. He had always been a practical man, the whole notion of dreams was new to him. He had reconciled himself to a solitary life, his friendships and his time and effort were absorbed in his increasingly demanding work. Now he was torn apart by impossible dreams. How could he criticize Olivia for a similar longing?

The old lady was watching him with sharp, amused eyes. The age difference between them was enough that she could have taught him as a schoolboy, and that might well be how she was regarding him now.

"She did not confide that in me," she responded. He knew it was her way of avoiding answering. And that meant that Olivia had loved the man as well as the adventure, but many things had made it impossible. Perhaps she had not even been asked.

How could the reality of Faraday, kind, honest but predictable, have matched the dream? It did not matter now, because Olivia had not gone, and she had refused Faraday, Newbridge, and John Barclay, and no doubt worn out her long-suffering brother.

He thanked Miss Mendlicott and left.

*F*ollowing the visit to Miss Mendlicott's, Runcorn went back to the vicarage, where he disturbed Costain preparing the next Sunday's sermon. The vicar looked tired and grieved, more as if he were searching for some thread of hope for himself than for others.

Runcorn felt a pang of compunction about disturbing him with questions that had to be painful, but such awareness had never hindered him before, and he could not allow it to do so now. There was a kind of comfort in duty.

"I don't know what further I can tell you," Costain said wearily. "Olivia could be exasperating, heaven knows, but I cannot imagine anyone being driven to such a rage as to do that to her. It was somebody quite mad. I just cannot think that anyone we know is so depraved."

"Such things are always hard to understand," Runcorn agreed. "But it is inescapable that someone did this." He had no time to spare on re-treading old ground, and there were no words that would change or heal anything. "I believe there was a young poet and explorer she was fond of," he said.

Costain frowned. "Percival? Interesting man, and knowledgeable, but hardly a suitor for Olivia. He spoke well. But that was two years ago at least. And he went to Africa, or maybe it was South America. I don't recall."

"Mountains of the Moon," Runcorn supplied.

"I beg your pardon?" Costain's voice was sharp, as if he suspected Runcorn of a highly insensitive flippancy.

"In Africa." Runcorn blushed. It was just the kind

of clumsiness Monk accused him of. "At least that is what I heard. Could such adventure have caught Miss Costain's imagination, and perhaps made her compare more realistic suitors with something unattainable?"

"Probably!" Costain ran his hands over his brow, pushing his hair back. "Perhaps. But what does that have to do with her death? They grew impatient with her. Faraday is now going to marry Mrs. Ewart, so I understand. Newbridge was annoyed because Olivia turned him down, but that is hardly a reason to lose his sanity altogether. He is a perfectly decent man. I've known him most of his life. His family has lived here for generations. He could find any number of other suitable young women. If you'll forgive me saying so, Mr. Runcorn, you are looking for violent passion where there is only irritation and inconvenience or, at the very worst, disappointment. I cannot help but think you are looking in the wrong places."

Runcorn had a deep fear that Costain was right. He was drawn to the emotions around Olivia and her betrothal, or lack of it, because he felt that was where the seat of much violence lay. Perhaps he only saw so much in it because he had fallen in love for the first time in his life.

But of course nothing would make him kill anyone over it, least of all Melisande. He wanted her happiness, he wished her to be loved and to marry a man worthy of her, which he did not consider Faraday was. But then, maybe he would never think any man worthy of Melisande.

He thanked Costain and asked to see his wife. With deep reluctance, permission was granted. Runcorn found himself in the sitting room opposite Naomi.

"Are you any closer to the truth, Mr. Runcorn?" she asked almost as soon as the door was closed. She spoke very quietly, as if she did not wish her husband to overhear her questions, or possibly Runcorn's answers.

"I am not sure," he replied honestly. "Miss Costain was not afraid of whoever killed her, until the very last moment, when it was too late. That suggests it was someone she knew, possibly even cared for. And it was a crime of great violence, so profound emotion was involved." He watched her face and saw the pain in it, so deep that guilt twisted inside him.

"You are saying it was someone who knew her well, and hated her." She stared out at the bare, winter garden and the tangled branches of the trees outlined against the sky. "She did awaken strange feelings in other people, sometimes unease, and a sense of loss for the unreachable. She was not content to be ordinary, but is that a sin?" She turned now to look at him, searching his eyes for a response. "She reminded us of the possibilities we have not the courage to strive for. We are too afraid of failure. Does one kill for that?"

"One can kill for safety," he answered, surprised at his own words. "Did she threaten someone's comfort, Mrs. Costain?"

She walked to the farther side of the window. "Not at all. It was a foolish thing to have said. I'm sorry. I don't even know what she was doing outside at that hour on a winter night. She must have quarreled with someone."

"Over what?" he asked. "Who would she meet in the churchyard? He came with a knife, as if he intended harm."

She winced and shivered, holding her arms around herself. "I have no idea."

He had a sharp sense that she was lying. It was nothing obvious, only a subtle tightness in her shoulders, an altered tone in her voice. Was she protecting her husband? Or even herself? Was the threat that Olivia posed far closer to home than anyone had previously thought? Had Olivia, in desperation, tried to force her brother into keeping her for the rest of his life, and had he found the endless, draining expense too much to endure? Had his tortured self-control broken, and had he seized a terrible escape? This situation answered every fact they knew.

But what secret? What did this quiet, sad, seemingly conventional house hide?

"I think you have an idea, Mrs. Costain," he told her. "You knew your sister-in-law as well as anyone did. You cared for her, and you understood her. You also must know the expense of her remaining unmarried, and refusing offer after offer for no reason she was prepared to give, unless it was to you?"

She turned around to stare at him, anger flaring in her eyes, her mouth hard. "If I knew who murdered Olivia, I would tell you. I do not. Nor do I know anything that would be of use to you. I have admitted that she was a disturbing person, and hard for many to understand. I can tell you nothing new. Please do not waste any more of your time, or mine, in asking me such things. Good day, Mr. Runcorn. The maid will show you out."

*H*ow dare you behave with such crass insensitivity?" Faraday accused him that evening when he answered his summons to the big house. They were standing in the library. The gas lamps were lit and a good fire roared and hissed in the grate.

"You will not approach Mrs. Costain on the subject again," Faraday went on. "If anything should be necessary to ask, I will do it. Have you no sense at all of how the poor woman must be feeling?" His face was red and his features pinched with anxiety and perhaps a sense of panic as failure crept closer around him. They knew nothing more than they had the morning after Olivia was found. Every thread they pulled came loose in their hands. But this was not Runcorn's jurisdiction, no one was going to blame him if Olivia's murder went unsolved. Faraday was the only one with something to lose.

"She is lying," he said aloud. "She knows something that could have provoked the kind of rage we saw in that murder."

"Dear God!" Faraday exploded. "Tell me you didn't say so to her!" He closed his eyes. "You did! Don't bother to deny it, it's in your face. You oaf!" Suddenly he was shouting, his voice raw. "This may be the way it is done in the alleys and brothels you usually police, but these are decent people, gentry, people of class and Christian values. Runcorn, the man's a vicar! Have you really no . . ." He drew in his breath and let out a heavy sigh. "No. I suppose you haven't. It was my failure that I even let you in at the door."

Runcorn felt as if the fire had burned out of the

grate to scorch him. Perhaps Faraday was right. He was clumsy, and had always lacked the grace of someone gifted like Monk. He had achieved his rank by plodding patience, determination, the will to succeed, and perhaps now and then a flash of understanding of how the poor and the frightened had found ways of retaliating. He kept his word, so people trusted him, but he was not a gentleman; he had never known how to be.

"I did not tell her she lied," he said quietly. "I said I believed she knew something relevant that she had not said. I think she is complaining so hard because that is true."

"Don't make it any worse!" Faraday begged. "Man, you are like a cart horse in the dining room. Just get out of it! God alone knows who killed Olivia Costain, but we aren't going to find out your way." His voice was rough with the edge of defeat. He must be hot standing in this room, so close to the fire, wearing his beautifully tailored jacket. It was of the best tweed, and cut with the casual elegance of one who does not need to impress.

And yet he did need to. The whole island was

watching him, waiting for him to take away the burden of fear and tell them it was over, and justice would be done. And he had no idea how to do it, that much was clear to Runcorn, even if not yet to anyone else.

And begrudgingly, Runcorn felt sorry for him. Not much is expected of ordinary men. There is room for failure. It costs, but it is a familiar part of life. In the extraordinary, the men of Faraday's privilege and office, it was crippling. The chief constable would not know how to deal with it. Nothing had prepared him for the bitterness or the shame of defeat. Probably all his life he had been expected to fill a certain mold, to win, to take pain or loss without complaint.

Did Faraday imagine that Melisande needed him to be faultless or she would not love him? Was that some legacy from his love of Olivia, or was it woven into his life and upbringing, inherited from his father, and his father before him? Did he think that if someone close to him, like a wife, were to know his weaknesses as well as his strengths, then they would use them to some kind of advantage, to manipulate or mock him?

No one can always be right. Every man has his flaws, the places where he is desperately vulnerable. Never to attempt anything that may cause pain, or defeat, is to be a coward at life. One loves those brave enough to try. Runcorn had seen women sometimes love the defeated far more tenderly, more passionately than the victor. To love is to protect, to nurture, to need, and in turn be needed.

How did he know that, and Faraday did not?

The silence had lengthened and Runcorn had not yet even tried to defend himself. "Then you had better look into the Costains yourself, sir," he said aloud. "Because there is much that she knows but will not tell me."

"Nonsense," Faraday replied. "Thank you for your help, but it is not proving of any use. You are free to leave Anglesey whenever you wish. Good day."

Runcorn was beyond the gates of the drive and into the road when Melisande caught up with him.

"Mr. Runcorn!"

He turned. They were level with the hedge now and hidden from the windows of the house. Maybe he would not see her many times more, certainly not alone. He stopped and faced her, trying to imprint on his mind every line of her brow, cheek, lips, the color and light of her eyes, so he would never forget.

"I heard Alan tell you to go," she said anxiously. "He does not realize how his voice carries. Please don't listen to him. He is frightened that none of us will solve this murder, and he will be blamed for that. He takes his responsibility very hard."

"He doesn't wish me to stay," he pointed out.

"Does that matter?" she asked. "He needs you to, we all do. Someone killed Olivia and we cannot turn away from that as if it were some force of nature, and not one of us. We will suspect each other, until we know."

"Do you know anything about the explorer she met about two years ago?" he asked. "Could she have loved him?"

She thought about it for several moments. "She never said anything to me, but then why should she? We spoke often. I liked her right from the first time we met, but we talked more of books, ideas, places, far more than of people we knew, and never of men."

Another darker thought occurred to Runcorn, but he could not mention anything so indelicate to Melisande, much less suggest it of a woman who had been her friend. He felt the heat on his skin even as he pushed the idea from his mind, although he could not dismiss it altogether.

"Do you think it is something to do with Reverend Costain?" Melisande asked. "Is that why you spoke to Naomi so bluntly?" She was trying to read Runcorn's face, perhaps judge from it what he was unprepared to say.

"I think Mrs. Costain may be trying to protect both her husband and Olivia," he replied, navigating a tenuous path between truth and lie. If Olivia were one of those rare women who prefer their own sex to the other, then it was an excellent reason why she would not wish to marry, and at the same time, it would be impossible for her to admit to it to anyone.

But what if someone had learned? Any man might feel unbearably betrayed to be rejected for another woman. It would be seen as the final insult. It would be unendurable if anyone else found out. Was that what the quarrel with John had been?

"Oh," she said softly, sensing the movement of his thought. "You do not need to be so delicate with me. I am aware of such things, in women as well as in men. But I had no sense that it was so with her."

Now the blood scorched up his face and he felt ridiculous. If Faraday, not to mention Barclay, knew that he had even entertained such a thought in Melisande's presence, let alone discussed it with her, they would be appalled.

She was smiling, a flicker of real amusement in her eyes. "I liked Olivia," she told him. "I felt comfortable with her, and very free to be honest, perhaps not only with her but with myself. And that is not always true for me. If I can bear the way she died, and think of the brutality, and the passion that caused it, then surely I can look at a little human frailty without turning away with thought only for myself? She deserved better than that of me. Moral queasiness is rather a cheap escape, don't you think?"

He looked at her, and for a moment the pity and the honesty in her face made her infinitely beautiful to him. Faraday, with his lumbering imagination and his simplistic judgments, was a clod, bitterly un-worthy of her.

He wondered again if she knew that Faraday had once courted Olivia also? Should he tell her? Was it just a grubby and horribly obvious attempt to spoil her happiness because he envied any man who could spend time in her company, let alone marry her? Or was it the only real honesty, because Faraday might be involved in Olivia's death?

He had no idea. The only answer would be to learn more about Faraday and then judge what to say. It must be the truth, and it must be fair. It was Melisande's safety that mattered, not whether she liked Runcorn's actions and certainly not whether Faraday did.

His face was still hot as he crafted his reply. "I don't like finding weaknesses in people, even if they help to solve a crime, but I can't afford to ignore them or lie to myself or others. I would like to have protected you from having to think of this."

"Thank you, Mr. Runcorn," she acknowledged. "I do not wish to be protected from life. I think we might miss a great deal more of the good, and the bad would find us anyway. At least the sense of emptiness would. I think I would rather eat something unpleasant now and then, than perish of starvation sitting at the table because I was afraid to try. Please find out what really happened to Olivia." She turned and walked away before he could find the words to answer her, and repeat his promise.

*H*e had no choice now but to look more deeply into Faraday's life and character. He began where Miss Mendlicott had ended and, through conventional methods, was able to look up the man's days in Cardiff University where he was moderately successful in gaining a degree in history, even though he did not need to earn his living by it. He had traveled in Europe on and off for a year or two in all the expected places. He did not see Venice or Capri. He did not venture as far as Athens, which Runcorn had read about, and would have leapt at the chance to see. He did not visit the beautiful city of Barcelona, named after Hannibal Barca, who had crossed the Alps with elephants, to attack Rome, before the days of Julius Caesar. That was one history lesson from school days that had fired Runcorn's imagination and he had never forgotten it.

Runcorn left the library in Bangor and walked out into the wind with his mind in a whirl. He had visited a different world where all the privileges of class and money did not buy the magic he had assumed. If Faraday had dreams at all, they were not of legendary places and the ghosts of the past. They seemed to be of the good opinions of others, perhaps domestic certainty and investment in the next generation of all that he had been bequeathed by his forebears.

As Runcorn walked down to the railway station he felt a sad, strange closeness to his subject. Faraday was in his early forties, and yet he wanted only safety, peace, and things to remain as they were.

Runcorn took the train to Caernarfon and continued his inquiries. He knew from long experience how to be discreet, to ask one thing while appearing to ask another. All he learned about Faraday confirmed the opinion that he was a decent man, but pedestrian, a man of likes and dislikes rather than of passions.

Runcorn remembered with a jolt that this was exactly how Monk had described him: half-hearted, lacking the fire or the courage to grasp for more than he could safely reach, a man who never dared the boundaries or stepped into the unknown as his bridges crumbled behind him. And Monk had despised him for it.

Did he now despise Faraday? Oddly, he did not. He pitied him and felt as if he were looking into a distorted mirror. There was something of himself in the man he saw, a man imprisoned in the expectations of others, too afraid of being disliked to follow his own vision, not hungry enough.

Did it take the face of one woman to stir a man deeply enough to abandon comfort and follow impossible dreams into the cold infinity? Then why was Faraday half-heartedly in love with Melisande, not absurdly and hopelessly as Runcorn was?

*T*he following day he stayed in Beaumaris and asked more questions, seemingly idling his time with local gossip and trivial pieces of information about the past.

To aid in this, he pretended to have come originally to Beaumaris to look at property, inventing a brother who had done well in trade in order to seem wealthy enough to do so.

He was shown a house in the neighborhood of Faraday's handsome home, which added little to his knowledge, but he learned more of Newbridge, since his house was within view across a stretch of sloping valley.

"Can't see it so well in the summer time," the estate agent, a Mr. Jenkins, pointed out.

"Yes. I see what you mean," Runcorn agreed. "Looks like quite a decent place. Might that be for sale, Mr. Jenkins?"

"Oh no, sir. That belongs to Mr. Newbridge. Been in his family for years."

"Big family, has he?" Runcorn asked innocently. "Good place for children, I imagine."

"No, not married yet," Jenkins replied.

"Betrothed, then?"

"Not as I know." Jenkins was keen for a sale. "Courting the vicar's sister, the poor young lady that was killed."

Runcorn looked skeptical. "Do you think Mr. Newbridge might sell, if the offer were good enough?"

"No sir, I don't. Money isn't everything."

"Looks like a lot of land for one man to handle, and in none too good repair." Runcorn squinted across the valley, the wind in his face. "Cause resentment, will it, if an outsider buys old land?"

"Yes sir, it could," Jenkins said candidly. "Newbridges've been here since the Civil War. Big thing to keep up, a position like this, being the last in the male line of the family an' all, but he'll soon find the right wife, and then there'll be sons to carry on."

Runcorn was struck with a sudden horror at the weight of such responsibility, the need to marry, the burden of expectation. Too many people cared what he did, were watching and needing him to produce sons and fill the demands of the future.

Was some of that why he responded badly to Barclay, and why he had taken Olivia's rejection with anger as well as disappointment? Had she said something about him that might make it even harder for him to find a wife who was willing and able to take up this enormous responsibility? Newbridge had no title, no hereditary office, not even great wealth—just a family name and land he was tied to by history. Was he always trying to keep up with other men he felt had more to give, more charm, more heritage, more hope of office in the future?

It would make him an easy mark for Barclay's cruelty.

"I think I'll wait until I've been in touch with my brother, thank you," Runcorn said to Jenkins. "I'll let you know."

$\mathcal{F}$araday sent for Runcorn that evening. He looked tired and disappointed, and even though he had demanded Runcorn's presence, he paced the carpet in front of the fire and seemed reluctant to broach the subject.

They spoke of trivialities. Outside the rain lashed at the windows and the wind was rising steadily, roaring in off the great sweep of the Celtic Sea.

Runcorn grew impatient. "If you've learned something, sir, and I can be of help, perhaps you'd tell me what it is."

Faraday winced at Runcorn's lack of polish, and instantly Runcorn felt gauche. He had a hideous vision of doing something appalling that he did not even understand until too late, and Melisande being ashamed of him. Except that that was absurd. She might be disgusted. But to be ashamed one had to care, to feel some kind of kinship with the one at fault.

Faraday was still pacing back and forth, lost in his own inabilities.

"You suggested that Miss Costain might have discovered something about her own family, a secret that was shameful or embarrassing," he began.

Runcorn was unhappy with the thought, but its

ugliness did not invalidate it. He was afraid that it could be true, and Naomi's strong, weary face filled his mind. "I thought of it as unlikely but not impossible," he conceded.

Faraday's voice was heavy. "I'm grateful for your professional skill, and glad I don't have to share the kind of experience that has given it to you."

In spite of the fire, Runcorn felt colder.

"You recognized a crime committed with intense hatred," Faraday continued. "I used to assume all murders were, but you exposed the difference for me to see. I should be obliged to you for that also, but I'm not sure that I am."

"Do you know something further?" Runcorn demanded, his voice betraying his emotion. "You didn't send for me in this weather to thank me for teaching you a part of your job you'll almost certainly never need again."

A slow stain of color spread up Faraday's cheeks. "Yes I do, but I have more yet to learn. Mrs. Costain is concealing something of which she is deeply ashamed, or if not ashamed, then at least terrified that it might become known. Costain's sister was slaughtered like an animal. This we all know." Faraday shifted his eyes. "And now it looks as if his wife might be an adulteress and have conceived to another man the child she never bore him." His voice choked with emotion, and for a moment he was unable to speak. His strong hands clenched at his sides until the knuckles shone white, and he could not keep them still.

Runcorn felt the wave of misery engulf him also. Had it been Olivia's own need for freedom which had driven her to confront Naomi, or the defense of her brother? Murder is never without pain, but this seemed even more steeped in it than most.

Faraday was staring at him still.

"What is it?" Runcorn demanded.

Faraday's voice was little more than a whisper, all but choking off at the end. "The baby is dead. It looks as if she killed him."

Runcorn was stunned, as if he had walked face-first into a wall and the pain of it dizzied his senses. Naomi Costain with her strange, powerful face, and a late-born, illegitimate child, which she had murdered with her own hands. Why? To hide her adultery? The obvious thought. But perhaps the child had been misshapen, abnormal? He found himself blinking and his throat inexplicably tight and rough. Could that be forgiven, such a helpless child robbed of life? Or snatched from pain? Or was she only saving herself, her humiliation? And then to be faced with blackmail by Olivia? "I can't do anything," he said aloud. "You'll need police authority to follow that." It was not cowardice speaking, even though he was glad he had no jurisdiction here.

"I'll get it for you," Faraday said hoarsely. "Please, Runcorn? These people are my friends, my neighbors. I have no idea how to deal with a crime like this."

Runcorn almost wanted to remind Faraday that it was he who had discovered this element of tragedy while Runcorn had not even guessed at it. He had talked with Naomi and seen nothing of this in her, no unfed hunger that consumed all honor and loyalty, no loss of her only child to whatever brutal end. His professional skills had failed him completely.

And it was Faraday, whose profound judgment he so despised, who had seen the answer. Faraday, who was going to marry Melisande.

He should be grateful, for her sake, that he was not the fool Runcorn had thought him. If he loved her, he was no fool.

He knew this thought should comfort him as he walked away down the hill, wind harder and traces of snow making a flurry of white in the gloom.

*D*uring the night the sense of his own failure deepened. He had come to Anglesey a stranger. He loved the vast silence disturbed only by the wind and the echo of waves on the shore. People here spoke more slowly, and there was a lilt of music in their voices, but he knew now that he only imagined he understood them. He had been as wrong as possible, not only about Olivia, who may have threatened to expose her own family, but also about Naomi, whom he had believed so strong but who had betrayed her husband, then her child, and finally Olivia. The one skill he believed he possessed had left him.

How did Faraday know about Olivia? Had Naomi admitted anything? Runcorn would not leave it like this, so many questions unanswered, so many of his own impressions mistaken.

As soon as he had dressed and had breakfast, he walked across the crisp frost and the pale fingers of new snow whitening the windward sides of the uneven ground. Far in the distance Snowdonia gleamed white.

He was admitted to the vicarage straight away, and Naomi came to the morning room where he had been asked to wait. He rose to his feet as she closed the door behind her and invited him to be seated again.

"Good morning, Mr. Runcorn," she said gravely.

He struggled to remove all emotion from his face, even his voice. He was unnaturally stiff, but he could not help it. Defeat and an overwhelming sense of loneliness almost choked him.

"Good morning, Mrs. Costain." What could he say

to her that was not absurd? Obviously Faraday had not spoken to her yet. She was almost at the end, and she had no idea. Within months she could be hanged.

"What can I do for you? There is nothing further I can tell you." Her face was bland, polite, not exactly at peace, but less scoured with grief than before, as if she were beginning to come to terms with the murder. Was she denying to herself what she had done, or was she merely a superb actress?

"Miss Costain had three suitors that I know of, ma'am: Mr. Faraday some time ago, then Mr. Newbridge, and most recently Mr. Barclay. She declined them all. Did you favor any of those for her?"

"No," she said easily. "I had no desire that she should marry without love. Mere affection would never have been enough for Olivia. She would have been wretched with a good but tepid man like Alan Faraday. It would have made them both unhappy, because he would have been aware of his failure to please her and it would have both confused and hurt him. She was not wise enough to know how to hide it. Melisande Ewart is gentler, much older within herself. She will probably accept the inevitable and if she has tears of despair, she will hide them from him. She is also, I think, kinder than Olivia. She will bring out the best in Alan, and he will never know it was she who did it, nor will she ever say so."

Runcorn was overtaken with a sense of loss, as if he were exiled far from all light and fire and the sound of laughter. He was too numb even to answer her.

"Newbridge is a good man, so far as I know," she went on gravely, almost as if she were speaking as much to herself as to him. "But I cannot say that I like him. My husband chides me now for it. But regardless, I had no wish that Olivia should marry him if she did not wish to. He wants many children, in order to establish his family again. I am not sure Olivia wanted to be that kind of woman. If you are devoted to a man then it is a pleasure and a privilege to work beside him, but if you are not, it is an imprisonment, a lifelong denial of yourself."

In his mind's eye he saw the woman in green who had walked past, her head high, and he almost was glad she had escaped these loveless fates. Then he realized what he was thinking, and who had brought him to that vision, and he was disgusted with himself. What had happened to his basic instincts?

"And as for John Barclay," Naomi went on. "Olivia did not refuse him, it was he who rejected her, suddenly and very bluntly." Now there was pain in her voice, but not the anger Runcorn would have expected. It was like an old wound reopened, not the outrage of a new one. Again he had the certainty that there was something profound about Olivia that this woman was hiding from him, perhaps from everyone.

"Did she know Mr. Barclay before this recent courtship?" he asked, the matter suddenly urgent.

Now the anger was there in her eyes, blazing up for an instant. "No," she said without hesitation. "Why do you ask?"

"It seems . . . brutal, if she did not rebuff him."

"It was," she agreed with a twist of her mouth. "But I do not think John Barclay is a nice man. He did not love Olivia, he wanted her, as a collector wants a rare and beautiful butterfly, to preserve it, not for its happiness. He will be content to put a pin through its body and capture its colors forever in death."

Runcorn remembered Olivia's body on the graveside, stained with blood, and thought for a moment that he was going to be sick.

"I'm sorry," Naomi said very quietly. "That was a bad thing for me to say. I apologize for it. Perhaps my grief is not as well-controlled as I imagined. Please forgive me."

Faraday was wrong, he had to be. There was a deeper answer to find. Perhaps he, too, was trying to protect Melisande from the fact that her brother was a cruel and manipulative man. But Runcorn knew that it could not be done. No matter how much you love, covering evil and allowing the innocent to walk in the shadow of blame is not a path you can take. There is no light at the end of it.

"Thank you, Mrs. Costain," he said gently. "Anger is like a knife, it can be dangerous when out of control, but you need it sometimes, to cut away what must go."

Her eyes widened with a flare of surprise. "Are you still working on the case, Mr. Runcorn? I thought you had given up. I'm so glad I was mistaken." The shadow was still there across her face; the lie she clung to.

"Yes. I'm still working," he said, knowing that that, at least, was true.

*D*isliking every step of it, Runcorn traced Barclay's actions over the last days before Olivia's death. It was not easy to be discreet, but it was a skill he had learned over his professional life. Barclay had clearly shown a great curiosity about Olivia. He was courting her, in rivalry with Newbridge, and it was natural that he should seek to know all he could about her, following her journeys.

Then it grew clearer as he asked questions, heard descriptions, that it was actually Naomi whose actions he was following, she in whose travels, whose expenditures he showed such an interest, not Olivia.

Runcorn's mind whirled. What had Barclay been seeking? He had come here to Caernarfon asking questions about Naomi, looking for times and dates, patterns of behavior. He had visited a hotel, a church which led him to a hospital, a quiet doctor with a small, expensive practice. Runcorn went to see Dr. Medway, inventing an excuse, and found a handsome man in his fifties, courteous and distinctly uncommunicative.

Was it possible Faraday was right after all? An illegitimate child fitted all these facts and places. In the later stages Runcorn learned that Olivia had come with her sister-in-law.

Why had she come? Had Naomi been desperate, perhaps heavy with child and in need of help? Had she trusted the one person on earth she should not have?

Except how could her husband not have known? Were they really so distant? What ice was in that house, or what storms, in those days?

All this happened some time after Olivia had sought refuge in friendship with the explorer poet, and longed to go with him to Africa, or wherever it was he intended. Had she remained at home because it was impossible for a woman to go to such parts of the world? Had he simply not asked her? Or was it from a duty to look after her sister-in-law in terrible distress, and for the life of the child, if nothing else?

And then Naomi had killed the child anyway.

But how could Runcorn have seen nothing of that in their faces? Or was he looking at the whole thing from the wrong side? Maybe the love story was Olivia's, not Naomi's. The child was Olivia's, and it was Naomi who had protected her, and was still protecting her name, even after she was dead.

What had happened to the child? Was it not a far greater sin to kill a live child than to abort one before it was born? Abortion was dangerous for the mother, but so was birth.

He turned and walked into the wind, back to the doctor's house. He knocked on the door, in spite of the late hour. If he missed the last train and spent the night on this side of the strait, it was immaterial.

"Yes, Mr. Runcorn?" Dr. Medway said curiously.

Runcorn already knew what he meant to do. "I have a story to tell you," he said. "And it is necessary that you listen to what I say. If you are not free to comment, I will understand, but you know the truth of what is being said, and you may decide that I need to know the truth of what happened."

The doctor smiled. "In that case you had better come in."

Runcorn accepted swiftly, and over an excellent supper by the fire, he told Dr. Medway of Olivia's death, what he had deduced, and what was said or hinted at darkly.

"I see," Medway said finally, his voice carrying the weight of tragedy. "You understand I cannot betray confidences, Mr. Runcorn? I will tell you no names, nor will I confirm any."

"Yes," Runcorn agreed.

Medway's face was very pale. "The child died soon after birth. It was one of the most harrowing losses of my career. I fought all I could to save him, but it was beyond my skill, or I believe, anyone's. No one was to blame, least of all the mother."

Runcorn pictured Olivia, weeping over the baby for which she had paid so much to bring into the world. Perhaps Percival had been the man whom she had truly loved. She had given up going with him in order to carry and deliver the child, and yet the baby had died. Or perhaps he had not been worthy of her, had not loved her for more than the swift infatuation of the moment. Runcorn chose to believe the former.

Thank God Naomi had been there, so at least she had not been alone. And she was even now protecting Olivia's memory, even if narrow and vicious men like John Barclay were happy to malign her.

Of course! That was why he had quarreled with her and dramatically ceased to court her! Did he hate her for her pregnancy? She had, in his mind, deceived him, allowed him to believe she was fit for him to marry. Would she ever have told him? Or if he had not found out, might she have accepted his proposal? No. But did Newbridge know that? Or did he arrogantly imagine she was intent upon trapping him?

Had Newbridge known? Was that why he, too, had apparently lost interest in her? There was nothing to suggest he had suspected anything. Runcorn had found no trace of him in his pursuit of Naomi. If he had known, then could it be that Barclay had told him?

Why? He could have let Newbridge marry her, and told him afterwards. That would have been an exquisite revenge.

But upon whom? Newbridge! And it was Olivia who had deceived him. Runcorn had learned enough about the gentry to understand that if that had happened, Barclay himself might have suffered a certain ostracism. They would have closed ranks around Newbridge to protect him, here in Anglesey at least. But word would have spread. Faraday, soon to be Barclay's brother-in-law, would also have believed it a betrayal, and despised Barclay accordingly.

However, if Barclay told Newbridge beforehand, that could be regarded as the act of a friend, a warning in time. What would Melisande think of his warning? Runcorn was uncertain. To him it was an act of cruelty he found repellent, but then he had in his own mind seen so much of Melisande in Olivia, the same loneliness, the dreams that could never be realized, the hunger for something more than daily obedience to the expectations of those who loved them, protected them, and imprisoned them with failure to understand.

Or perhaps it was he who did not really understand. He confused the romantic with the real.

And he was still no closer to proving who had slashed Olivia with a carving knife in hatred for duping him, letting her believe she was all he wanted, when in fact he was nothing she wanted. Was it Barclay? Newbridge? He was terribly afraid that it was Barclay, and the revelation of it would hurt Melisande unbearably. It might even prevent her marriage to Faraday, or anyone else that could make her happy and safe.

What could Runcorn do to prove Barclay's innocence, that would not ruin Olivia's reputation and hurt irreparably the people who had loved her? And even showing Barclay innocent of murder could not conceal that his cruelty was self-serving and repellent.

He would start again with every detail about Barclay. It might be possible to prove that he could not have taken the knife from the kitchen and followed Olivia up to the graveyard, or perhaps that he could not have returned and changed his clothes, disposed of them without anyone knowing! Maybe he could prove no clothes were missing? It would be long and tedious, but for Melisande's sake it could be done.

It was now only three days before Christmas, but here there was no excitement in the air, no shouts of "Merry Christmas," or sounds of laughter. Even the smell of Christmas was blown away in the wind.

It took Runcorn two careful, unhappy days to ascertain that Barclay had learned enough of the story to be sure of the rest, and had certainly spoken alone with Newbridge just before Newbridge had been seen in such a rage as to be white-faced, and almost blind to those around him, two days before Olivia's death.

Runcorn felt gradually sicker with every new piece of information. It looked as if Barclay could have killed Olivia, and was carefully making it appear that Newbridge had.

In the evening he met with Faraday.

Faraday was angry and embarrassed, his face was pink not only from the warmth of the room, but from the high flush of emotion.

"You've been investigating John Barclay," he said as soon as Runcorn had closed the door. "For God's sake, man, if you felt you had to do it, could you not at least have been a little more careful? I told you he had discovered Mrs. Costain's secret, I didn't expect you to tread exactly in his footsteps, and then all but imply he was incriminated in it! He'd never even been to Anglesey at that time! What on earth are you thinking of?"

Runcorn was startled. Had he really been so clumsy that Barclay already knew he was pursued? Apparently. Or was it the suspicions of a guilty man, always looking over his shoulder because he expected pursuit?

The only honest answer now was to tell Faraday what he had learned.

When he finished, Faraday stared at him, all the hectic color drained from his face. "Are you certain of this, Runcorn?" he asked.

"I'm certain of all I've told you," Runcorn replied. "I'm not yet sure what it means."

"It means poor Olivia was killed for it," Faraday said sharply.

Runcorn was still standing, cold and unhappy, yet

again blocked from the fire by Faraday. "Yes, but by Newbridge, or Barclay?"

"Find out," Faraday commanded him. "And for the love of heaven, this time be discreet."

*I*n the morning, Runcorn left early to begin again. The ground was rock hard from the frost and the grass edges were white. Even so, Melisande was waiting for him at the end of the road. He barely recognized her at first; she was so closely wrapped within her cloak that it hid the outline of her body and shielded her face. She seemed to be staring towards the sea, until she heard his boots crunching the ice, then she turned.

"Good morning, Mr. Runcorn." Even in so few words her voice was sharpened with fear.

He felt that twist of emotion inside himself, but fiercer than before.

"Good morning, Mrs. Ewart." It would be absurd to ask her if she was waiting for him. There was no other reason she would be standing here growing steadily colder. He searched her eyes, wide and dark with dread.

She did not waste words. She was trembling with cold. "Alan told me that he had discovered why Mr. Newbridge abandoned Olivia so hastily, and why John also ceased to court her. I believe he told you also?" That was barely a question, but the disappointment was painful, a dull ache beneath the words.

Temptation surged up inside him to tell her that it was he, not Faraday, who had found the truth, but he did not want to tell her until he had proven that it was not Barclay who had killed Olivia, but Newbridge. He drew in his breath to explain, and realized how intensely such an explanation was for his own sake. It was not she whose heart he longed to ease, but his own, because she thought he had let her down. He wished her to think well of him. Vanity, and above all, his own hunger.

That was why Faraday had taken the credit for something he had not done, because he needed Melisande to think him cleverer than he was.

Runcorn took a deep breath and swallowed it down. "Yes," he said simply. "The child was hers. He died almost immediately, so she never needed to tell anyone else. And perhaps the loss was easier to bear if other people did not speak of it."

Melisande's eyes swam with tears. She struggled to speak and failed. Her pity for Olivia was so intense it drowned out even her fear for Barclay. For moments they stood there in the ice and the widening morning light, overshadowed by the same aching grief. The sun sparkled on the frost, as if the rough grass were encrusted with diamonds. In the distance the sea was flat calm, its surface disturbed only by currents and little ruffles of breeze, like the weft of silk.

"I wish I had known," Melisande said at length. "I would at least have told her that it made no difference to me. How terribly alone she must have been."

"Not alone," he said gently. "Naomi was always with her."

She turned to him, hope flaring up in her eyes. "Was she? Please don't tell me something to comfort me if it is not true. Please, always tell me the truth. I need one person who doesn't lie, however kind the reason."

"I won't lie," he promised rashly. He would have promised her anything. "Naomi never let her down."

She smiled slowly, a soft sadness filling her face, more beautiful to him than the radiance of the sun over the ground. "Thank you," she said sincerely. "I must go, before they ask me why my morning walk took so long. Please . . . please don't stop your search. It is too late now to hide anything." And without waiting for his answer, she walked with increasing speed up the hill back towards the great house.

Runcorn began straight away. He loathed Barclay and despised him for what he seemed to have done both to Olivia and to Newbridge, but still, he wanted to prove beyond all further question that he was not legally guilty of murder even if morally he was. That was a different issue and the law had no remedy for it.

Runcorn knew the date of the birth, it was a matter of tracing back to nine months before that. He was already convinced that Costain knew nothing about the child. His eagerness to marry Olivia to first Faraday, then Newbridge, and finally Barclay, meant that either he was unaware of her child and its death, or he was unbelievably insensitive. Runcorn was certain it was the former.

Still, he should ask Naomi again.

She received him in her own room in the vicarage, a quiet space on the ground floor filled with gardening gloves, secateurs, string, outdoor boots and trugs for carrying cut blooms and greenery. She was arranging a bowl of holly with berries the color of blood, small golden onions, and sprigs of leaves and evergreen that he could not name. Some leaves were dark red as wine, and the bowl glowed with purple, green, gold, and red. He admired it, quite honestly. There was a rich warmth to it, as if it proclaimed hope and abundance in a dark season.

He did not waste her time, or his own, with prevarication. "Do you know who was the father of Olivia's child, Mrs. Costain?"

"Yes," she said simply. "But it was no one you know, and I have no desire to tear up his emotions or ruin his reputation, so there is no purpose in your pursuing it. He never knew she was with child, and he is too far away from here to have had any part in her death."

"Percival, I assume," he concluded. "I had not thought it was Mr. Newbridge, but I needed to be certain."

"Newbridge?" she looked startled, almost amused. "Good heavens, no! Whatever made you imagine that?"

"You are perfectly sure?" he persisted.

"Perfectly," she said with feeling. "But if you doubt me, you can prove it for yourself. He was away in England at the time, Wiltshire, I think. Certainly he was miles from here. He was staying with his sister, and buying cattle, or something of the sort. At that time he was more concerned with improving his livestock than gaining a wife."

"What sort of man was Percival?" Another idea was gaining strength in his mind.

She smiled, placing a last golden onion in its place to complete the light and shade of the arrangement.

"I never thought of using onions like that," he said.

"One uses what one has," she replied. "And onions

keep very well. What was he like? He was fun, full of ideas, an imagination which could make you laugh and cry at the same time. He was not particularly handsome, but his face was unique, and he had a smile that lit up his eyes and made you feel as if you could survive anything as long as he liked you."

"And did he like Olivia?" He did not want to hear that he had not. But if it had been true, he had to know.

Naomi looked away. "Oh yes, as much as she loved him, I think. But he was young and poor, a dreamer. It will be years before he can afford to marry, if ever. And he was not suitable for a girl of Olivia's breeding. My brother would look far higher than a penniless wanderer for her. My mother-in-law was a lady," she added. "Very little money, but a heritage back to Norman days." She sighed. "Which is slightly absurd, since if you think about it, we must all have a heritage back to Eve, or we would not be here. I don't give a fig who my ancestors were, only what I am, because that I can do something about."

Runcorn stared at her.

She looked back levelly. "Are you asking me if

Olivia could or would have married him? She would have, but he had more sense than to ask her. Newbridge did, and she refused him. Kindly, I hope."

There it was, as clear as it would ever be. Newbridge had offered her all he had, and she had refused him. And John Barclay had told him that she had been willing to lie with an explorer with neither land nor family, and to bear his illegitimate child. To Newbridge that must have been the ultimate insult, not only to his love but to all his lineage, his values, and his manhood. It remained now only to trace his exact actions on the night of her death, perhaps even to find the knife, or prove from where it was missing, or the clothes he had worn, and probably destroyed.

These were things Faraday had the power to do. Runcorn thanked Naomi and left, out into the day so cold the air stung his skin and the breath of the wind was like ice between the folds of his scarf.

*F*araday conducted the search and found the last pieces, as Runcorn had suggested. The knife was hidden in one of the barns. It took great care, but traces of blood were found, and Trimby agreed that the blade's shape matched the wounds. More incriminating than that, they found the ashes of the clothes Newbridge had worn that night. There were not sufficient remains to identify them, but the suit in question was gone and Newbridge could not explain its absence. He might have considered claiming to have given it to someone, but there was no one to substantiate it. The truth was terribly and agonizingly clear.

By mid-morning Newbridge was arrested and taken to the police cells in Bangor. Faraday told the waiting journalists and the public, briefly and with dignity, that the case was over, and justice would be done. The truth would be told at trial in due course. For now, the solution was plain, and he spoke for Olivia's family and for all the people of Anglesey when he reminded them that tomorrow was Christmas Day. He asked for respite so they might all, for a brief time, remember the season and give thanks for the birth and life of Christ, and the hope of forgiveness and renewal in the world.

Runcorn stood in the crowd and felt the surge of

gratitude that some kind of resolution had been reached, and there was justice and healing ahead. The admiration for Faraday was palpable, a new respect for more than the office. This was for the man himself, and the patience and skill he had shown. They believed in him. They would not forget this, please heaven, the most horrific case Anglesey would ever know.

Not once did Faraday mention Runcorn's name, let alone suggest that he had been the one to find the solution.

Runcorn separated himself from the crowd and walked away towards the wide sweep of the water. The sun, low in the west, made the great span of the bridge look like black fretwork on the sky across the burning colors of the sunset-painted water.

He would leave now. Melisande was as safe as he could make her. Barclay was shallow and manipulative, a man of innate cruelty, but Faraday would protect her from the worst of that. It was the best he could hope for. At least now Faraday would not have to prove himself any more. There must be a certainty that he had succeeded and so Barclay would be held back from ever criticizing him. Runcorn could hardly do anything but give his blessing to the marriage.

The wind stung Runcorn's eyes and he blinked hard. He refused to acknowledge, even to himself, that he was crying. But he was smiling as well. It was he who had solved the case, he who had found justice for Olivia, and some kind of safety for Melisande. She would never know Faraday had not been as inquisitive, or as successful, as he allowed people to suppose.

Runcorn was second fiddle, never first, but he had played the more beautiful tune. He had allowed himself to be guided by his emotions, and that was something he had never done before. This great clean land and water, with its light, its horizon beyond dreaming, had made a better man of him. He did not need anyone else to reassure him of that. He would carry it away with him, a better gift for Christmas than all the wealth, the food, the colors, or the rejoicing.

"Mr. Runcorn."

He turned around slowly. Melisande was standing on the quay behind him, the wind in her hair and the sunset light on her face. He gulped, all his resolve blown away in a single instant.

"Thank you," she said gently. Her cheeks were burning, more than the fire on the water could reflect. "I know it was you who worked out who killed Olivia, and why. And I know my brother well enough to guess at the part he played. I long ago ceased to believe he was a nice person, but I am grateful that you tried to protect me from knowing the extent of his cruelty."

He could still think of nothing to say. He wanted to tell her that he loved her, he would always love her, and no price to his own pride or ambition was too great to pay for her happiness. But that would only embarrass her, and forfeit the last, brief thread of friendship that they had, which he could keep bound to his heart.

"You gave Alan all the pieces, didn't you?" she asked.

He would not answer. It was the last temptation, and he refused to succumb. He smiled at her. "He's going to make a good policeman."

"I hope so," she agreed. "I think it matters to him.

But he is not as good as you are, because there will probably never be another case like this." She took a deep breath and let it out slowly. "And he is not as good a man as you are. Truth means less to him, and he does not seek it for its own sake."

He felt his cheeks burn. He would never in all his life forget this moment. From now on, forever, he would strive to be the man she had said he was to her. He wanted to tell her how great a gift that was, that the fire of it burned inside him, lighting every corner, every wish and thought, but there were no words big enough, gracious enough, articulate enough to do this feeling justice.

"Mr. Runcorn," she said impatiently, her face burning. "Do I have to ask you if you love me? That is so undignified for a woman."

He was stunned. She knew. All his careful concealment, his efforts to behave with dignity had been for nothing.

"Yes," he said awkwardly. "Of course I do. But—"

"But you don't want a wife?"

"Yes! Yes, I do . . . but . . ."

He was paralyzed. This was not possible.

She lowered her eyes and slowly turned away.

He took a step after her, and another, catching her arm gently, but then refusing to let go. "Yes, I do, but I could not marry anyone else. Every time I looked at her, I would wish she were you. I've never loved before, and I cannot again."

She smiled at him. "You don't need to, Mr. Runcorn. Once will be enough. If you would be so good as to ask me, I shall accept."

ABOUT THE AUTHOR

ANNE PERRY is the bestselling author of four earlier holiday novels—*A Christmas Journey, A Christmas Visitor, A Christmas Guest,* and *A Christmas Secret*—as well as two acclaimed series set in Victorian England—the William Monk novels and the Charlotte and Thomas Pitt novels—and five World War I novels. Anne Perry lives in Scotland. Visit her website at www.anneperry.net.

ABOUT THE TYPE

This book was set in Century Schoolbook, a member of the Century family of typefaces. It was designed in the 1890s by Theodore Low DeVinne of the American Type Founders Company, in collaboration with Linn Boyd Benton. It was one of the earliest types designed for a specific purpose: the *Century* magazine, maintaining the economies of a narrower typeface while using stronger serifs and thickened verticals.